AFRICAN WRITERS SERIES LIST

Founding editor · Chinua Achebe

D1133511

AFRICAN WRITERS SERIES
152
The Stone Country

The Stone Country

ALEX LA GUMA

HEINEMANN
LONDON · IBADAN · NAIROBI · LUSAKA

Heinemann Educational Books Ltd
48 Charles Street, London W1X 8AH
P.M.B. 5205, Ibadan · P.O. Box 45314, Nairobi
P.O. Box 3966, Lusaka
EDINBURGH   MELBOURNE   AUCKLAND
TORONTO   HONG KONG   SINGAPORE
KUALA LUMPUR   NEW DELHI

ISBN 0 435 90152 4

© 1967 Alex La Guma
First published by Seven Seas Books, Berlin 1967
First published in African Writers Series 1974

Printed Offset Litho and bound in Great Britain
by Cox & Wyman Ltd, London,
Fakenham and Reading

Dedicated to
the daily average of 70,351 prisoners
in South African gaols in 1964

While there is a lower class, I am in it.
While there is a criminal element, I am of it.
While there is a soul in jail, I am not free.

EUGENE DEBS

PART I

1

"I reckon we won't be out for Christmas," George Adams said.

The boy said nothing.

They were alone. George Adams stood at the door and gazed out, his back to the boy. The upper half of the door was a barred window covered with tough wire mesh. Outside the door was a concrete gallery running the length of the top floor of the Isolation Block, and at the end of it concrete steps, juxtaposed to the gallery, led down to the ground floor. In the wall against the stairs was another window which looked out onto a rectangle of asphalt which was all that could be seen of the outer square. The patch of asphalt was sunlit, as if it was being seen through a yellow pane.

George Adams felt in his shirt pocket for a cigarette and lighted it. He blew a plume of smoke, watched it disintegrate against the wire screen and drift out over the gallery.

"What you reckon the time is now?" the boy, who was called The Casbah Kid, asked.

"I don't know," George Adams said. "Must be past three." And then he remembered that the boy behind him would probably never see the outside world again, or have to bother about time.

"Almost bleddy supper time, and we with three meals off," the boy said. He had a cold, impersonal voice coming from below a raw and swollen lip.

"Well, we'll be getting it back tomorrow, hey," George Adams told him. "Eating that pap again. You hungry?"

"They can shove their cat-head," the boy muttered.

He spoke seldom and reluctantly, as if he was always conscious of the sound of what he said. But lately, alone with the other man, he had opened up a little. Getting him to talk was like prying open the jammed door of a vault.

They had not eaten all day, having been deprived of three meals, and George Adams was feeling somewhat hungry. He guessed that the boy was hungry too, but that he would not admit it. George Adams thought, Well, it's not as if you're missing Sunday dinner at home.

It was warm in the cell, and the boy was sprawled on his back on a rope mat and an old, worn blanket, dressed only in his shabby, stained jeans and gym shoes. Around them the walls were grimy, battleship-grey halfway up, and a dirty yellow-white above, all the four surfaces covered with inscriptions scratched into the paint or written in black pencil; the usual prison litany of man's inhumanity to man: *Gus was here for Housebreak and Theft; Johnny Bril you are a pig; I'll never see blue skies again; The Buster Boys was here; Never trust a woman she will make you sorry; 22 May Willy King got 4 years for rape; This guy is going to swing – so what?*

Interspersed among these were drawings of over-developed nude women, surprisingly artistic examples of still life in black and white, and numerous supplications to God for mercy. Twentieth century man forced back to the cave.

Somewhere outside, a leaking pipe dripped with infinite reluctance.

George Adams turned from the metal-clad door and went over to his own sleeping-mat, and sat down on it, his back against the scribbled wall. He was a short man with a skin the colour of an old penny and dark, curly hair, a slightly Negroid face with thick black eyebrows meeting above his nose, while his eyes were deep-set and friendly, bright as polished coins.

He was about to pinch out the cigarette into the sardine can they used as an ashtray, but changed his mind and gestured with the butt towards the boy.

"Want a puff?"

"T'anks."

"Watch out for your lip."

"Is okay."

The boy did not move, except to reach for the butt, and lay there looking at the ceiling, blowing smoke.

Somewhere a man started to sing *Nearer my God to Thee,* in a sad and emotion-laden voice that broke through the general silence.

The boy said with mild contempt, through the ragged veil of smoke:

"Hymns." Then he asked grudgingly, "You worried about being in over Chris'mas?"

George Adams smiled, and said: "Not really. But it would be nice to be with a man's family, *mos*. People have a good time."

"*Ja,* get drunk. Go to church. You go to church, mister?"

"Hell, I never been in church since I was a *pikkie*."

The boy crushed the last of the cigarette and then got up, walked over to the stainless-steel urn in a corner and ran water into a tin mug. He said, between sips, "Heaven and hell. I don't give a damn where I go when they swing me." He spoke without expression, his voice as impersonal as a loudspeaker announcement at a railway station.

George Adams looked at The Casbah Kid and felt a pang. The convict was still singing the hymn, somewhere beyond them in another part of the world. The boy put down the mug and came back to his mat, dabbing the damaged lip carefully on the back of his hand.

He was nineteen and he had had his hair cropped short, so that with his slight, wiry figure, he looked like a picture of a Japanese prisoner of war. He even had a wispy, youthful moustache across the swollen upper lip.

He dropped down on the bedding again, and scratched his armpits. George Adams looked at him, and then asked softly: "Don't it worry you, old son?"

"Whatter?"

"I don't mean about heaven and hell. But ... but ..." He did not want to say it. "If they ...."

The Casbah Kid said, "Like if they give me the rope?"

"Well, *ja*, man."

"Crack. Look, mister, you going to die someday, don't I say? We all got to die. Hear me, mister, I put a knife in a *juba*. He went dead. Is put out, like. Everybody got his life and death put out, reckon and think." He bit at a finger-nail and looked at it. "Like me and you, and ... and that basket, Butcherboy."

"Put out?" George Adams asked. "You reckon so? Man, if our life was laid out for us beforehand, what use would it be for us to work to change things, hey?"

"Right, mister. You can't change things, *mos*." He chewed the cuticle of a thumb.

"But hear me, chommy. People's trying to change things all the time."

"*Ja*. So what do they get? Crack."

George Adams looked across at the boy and shook his head sadly. He said, "Maybe is too late, but don't you feel sorry about that one you stabbed?"

The boy looked at him. "What one? Oh, him. Sorry? What is sorry? I tell you, mister, his death was put out for him. There is me in this subway, hear me, hey. And this john come along, drunk likely. So I stop him and try to go through his pockets. He got this wake-up gold wrist-watch on, too, hey. But he don't give up straight. He want to

14

struggle, *mos*. So the next thing the knife is in him. They catch me three weeks after, up the line, and they find the watch on me. Okay, mister, I'm not squealing. It was put out, don't I say?"

"But, listen –"

The Casbah Kid broke in surlily: "Forget it, mister. You's clever. You got things to talk about, and brains. Okay. But leave it, hey. Me, I'm going to swing. Who cares? My old man was hanged, so what about it?"

George Adams said: "Your father? Your pa?"

But The Casbah Kid had turned away onto his side, facing the wall, withdrawing into stubborn silence.

The hymn-singer had now switched to *We plough the fields and scatter the good seeds on the ground*. Behind and below the block, where the kitchen was situated, other sounds were intervening. A lid clanged and voices called out: "Three hundred and sixty-five Coloured remands. You got that pap for the Bantus? Twenty-three pox yard. Hard labours all ready?" The hymn-singer was still holding forth when the sudden voice of the guard shouted at him to shove his mouth somewhere. There came the sounds of heavy doors being unlocked, and then the distant muttering of many voices, like the far-away bleating of sheep, as prisoners were released from rows of cells to collect their supper.

George Adams lay on his blanket and considered the strange boy opposite him, whose father had been hanged.

2

The steel prison truck swayed and threw the men packed into it against each other, so that elbows jabbed ribs and faces and everybody cursed. Eventually the truck settled down to a steadier drive and some of the men broke into song. They were jammed tight into the back of the big steel vehicle, crowded onto the metal benches along each side, packed in on the floor, and still more stood awkwardly among those squatting, clinging to the iron ribs of the canopy. It was hot in the truck too, and the air was heavy with the smell of cramped bodies and sour breath and unwashed clothes.

George Adams had climbed in first, and so was jammed into a corner behind the driving-cabin, trapped by a rockfall of grimy muscles and smelly clothing, butting knees and squirming feet. All around him was a composition of faces, old faces, young faces, middle-aged faces; faces burned with stubble or cicatriced with scars; bloated faces and depraved faces; vicious faces and kind faces; faces hopeless, impersonal, happy, frightened, brutal. It was as if all the experiences of mankind had been thrust into these few cubic yards of steel-confined space. Almost everybody was singing now. Others peered through the ventilator slits in the walls of the truck and yelled and whistled at glimpses of the world outside. Everybody singing, whistling, shouting, created a block of solid sound. The truck turned a corner, swaying again, and the squirming mass of men crowded tighter, curses punctuating the singing.

Looking at the faces about him, George Adams thought that he could do with a bath. He felt sweaty, and he hadn't shaved for days; his mouth tasted coppery. He could do with a bath, he thought. It was funny, thinking about a bath. "Taking a bath" was underworld slang for going to prison. He wanted a smoke, too, but he was jammed tight and could not move his hands to his pockets to find the cigarettes. He could not see Jefferson.

A face grinned at him, showing greenish, carious teeth in a wrinkled, mud-brown face. The face yelled at him, sending a horrid blast of breath into his.

"Is okay, man. Is okay. Not to worry, don't I say?"

"Is okay," George Adams smiled back at the face. It nodded, grinning. George Adams wondered what crime this one had committed.

The truck pushed on, and then, gears grinding with the sound of violated metal, slowed down and finally came to a stop. The drive from the courts to the prison had taken about fifteen minutes, and now the singing dwindled and bodies were prepared for release from cramp.

The prison overlooked the city and the harbour, a squat, wide girdle of brownstone and grey-painted mortar and concrete enclosing a straining body of brickwork and more stone.

It had been built in the last century, during Victorian times, and over the years bits and pieces had been added to its interior, alterations made here and there, and because it could not expand outwards, it had closed in upon itself in a warren of cells, cages, corridors and yards.

Outside, the façade had been brightened with lawns and flower-beds: the grim face of an executioner hidden behind a holiday mask. The brasswork on the castellated main door was polished to perfection, and the flagged pathway up to it, kept spotless, as if at any moment it would receive some dignitary or other. It waited like a diseased harlot, disguised in finery, to embrace an unsuspecting customer.

The truck had backed up close to the great wood-and-metal side gate, and now the men inside could hear the padlocks on the truck's rear door being unfastened. A murmur of expectancy jumped from mouth to mouth, and then the doors were jerked open and there was the khaki-uniformed guard looking in at them, one hand holding the door and the other grasping a thick sheaf of admission forms. Another guard, wearing a holstered pistol, stood on the other side of the door.

The one holding the door shouted, "Come, come, come."

The prisoners surged and then, one by one, bounded down the metal step from the truck and through the open door in, the huge gate, while the guards counted them off.

George Adams pushed past those who, for some reason, waited to get out last, and was glad for the feel of fresh air in his lungs. He jumped down from the truck and crossed the threshold of the door. A guard with a big key in one hand, inside the gate, counted him off. This man was lean and his pink face was thin and hard as the edge of a pot-lid, and his eyes revealed no expression as his lips moved monotonously with the counting.

". . . . twenty-three, twenty-four . . . . thirty-one . . . ."

His key stroked the air as he counted, like an iron appendage of a robot.

". . . . thirty-eight, thirty-nine . . . ."

Beyond this guard was a grille of steel bars running from wall to wall, cutting off the gateway from the entrance yard, and another guard with a key stood by a gate in the grille, re-counting the prisoners who stepped through.

In the entrance yard in front of the Reception Hall, more warders waited, and Coloured long-term convicts in canvas trousers and navy-blue jerseys, who shouted, "Fall in, fall in. Two-two. Two-two." They shouted to exert the precarious authority bestowed upon them by their watchful masters, and pushed and bullied the shuffling prisoners into a double column, snapping like leashed dogs.

Inside the yard, past the iron grille and the gate, the atmosphere had suddenly chilled, as if the afternoon had suddenly been cut off. The shadows of the stone walls on each side of the area made a greyness that was as threatening as the expressionless faces of the flat-capped warders whose frigid eyes watched for the slightest suspicion of indiscipline.

Guards and prisoners, everybody, were the enforced inhabitants of another country, another world. This was a world without beauty; a lunar barrenness of stone and steel and locked doors. In this world no trees grew, and the only shade was found in the shadow of its cliffs of walls, the only perfume it knew came from night-soil buckets and drains. In the summer it broiled, and it chattered in the winter, and the only music the regulations allowed was composed out of the slap-slap of bare feet, the grinding of boots, counterpointed by shouted orders, the slam of doors and the tintinnabulation of heavy keys. Anything else smacked of rebellion.

When the prisoners had fallen in in twos, a guard holding the sheaf of admission forms began yelling out names from them, and one by one they answered and dashed for the entrance to the Reception Hall. Those who seemed too slow were urged on with a slap or a shove from a long-timer or a shout from another guard.

".... James Hannes ...."

"Old *baas*."

"Phillip Martin ...."

"*Ou baas*."

".... Henry Sampson ...."

"Here I am, boss."

Ragged street-corner hoodlums, shivering drunks, thugs in cheap flamboyant clothes and knowledgeable looks, murderers, robbers, housebreakers, petty criminals, rapists, loiterers and simple permit-offenders, tumbled in a line through the doorway.

Once the guard with the papers stumbled over an African name, and when the man hesitated he was stormed at with an avalanche of insults and abuse.

"Come on, you – – – – kaffir. Do you think this is a – – – – location?"

".... Anthony Langeveldt ...."

"*Baas*."

"Samuel Prince."

"My *baas*."

"William Papagaai."

"That's me."

"What kind of a blerry name is that? Christ, you look like a – – – – parrot."

The prisoner laughed ingratiatingly and others joined in with a murmur of hesitant glee.

"Shut your – – – – mouths, you *bliksems*. You reckon this is a – – – – circus?"

Silence fell again, and the guard scowled, red-faced, at the lines, and then returned his eyes to the wad of papers in his thick, pink hands.

George Adams moved up next to Jefferson and tugged at his sleeve, whispering, "Here we are, brother."

"Ha, it is nothing," Jefferson whispered back. "I was through all this before. During the Emergency."

"We won't be together, will we?"

"No. Sorry. This jail is a small something of what they want to make the country. Everybody separate, boy: White, African, Coloured. Regulations for everybody, and a white boss with a gun and a stick." He chuckled, showing his white teeth.

Jefferson was the same height as George Adams, but heavier. Two bright eyes, restless geckoes, jumped in his wide African face. "But it's going to be okay, boy. The hell with them."

"*Ja*, the hell with them," George Adams replied. But his heart skipped when he heard his name shouted, and he blundered forward after the man ahead of him. He was aware of the beating of his heart as he walked swiftly through the doorway and down a narrow corridor paved with worn flagstones in pink and white. The stones gave way to worn boards and another corridor and there was the smell of dust and mustiness in the air. Then he was in a large hall with a wooden floor and grey walls and shelves containing great, flat record books, and a counter along one side of the hall.

Against the wall the prisoners were crowded together, shuffling, muttering, and behind the counter uniformed clerks and two white trusties were writing, examining piles of forms, or paging through huge books. Behind George Adams other prisoners were coming in, crowding him into the jam ahead.

His heart had ceased thumping, but the apprehension was still there, so that now he felt like an immigrant entering a new and strange country, wondering what was going to happen to him. Then he blotted out the feeling, shutting the door of his mind on it, condemning it and locking it away. It's like learning to swim for the first time, he thought. The first shock of the ice-cold water, and then you settle down to keep your head above the surface.

He looked back, craning his neck, to peer over the heads behind him, feeling the gust of sour breath from the man nearest him, and looked for Jefferson again. George Adams saw him near the back of the crowd, and Jefferson seeing him in turn, grinned and raised a thumb in salute.

Now the sheaf of admission forms was in the hands of another warder, one of the clerks, who stood at the counter while a trusty inked a flat block with a roller, getting ready for the taking of finger-prints. Each prisoner admitted into the jail had to have his thumb-prints recorded on his form; so the shouting of names started all over again.

"Sulehman Adams . . . ."

"My baas."

The man jumped forward and the guard took first one wrist, and then the other, snapping at him to let his fingers go limp. First one thumb-print, and then the other was impressed on the paper, and the prisoner was directed to another part of the Reception Hall.

"Samuel De Bruyn."

"Ou baas."

"Albert March."

"John Solomons . . ."

"There's water!"

And a little man skipped forward in a half-clownish, half-derisive dance of an old lag, and had his thumb-prints taken. He rubbed the black ink casually into his hair and headed towards a wide archway with two steps which led down to the Property Room.

"Where the – – – – ing hell you think you going?"

"Oh, my boss, is *mos* right, don't I say?"

"– – – – off back where you came from, you *donder*."

The little man shuffled back to join the other men, winking at them and grinning sheepishly.

"Joseph Ackerman . . . ."

"Right."

"Titus Beekman."

"My crown!"

Some of those waiting were conversing in whispers.

"I say, is Gorilla Abrams still in the remand?"

"Nay, man. Got nine to fifteen last month."

"Where you sleeping?"

"In the *Groot Kamer*, the Big Room."

"You can't, man. You a admission. Got to go with the others."

While all this was happening, those who had been sentenced by the courts had been called aside and made to strip, and they stood in a bunch, stark naked, each holding his bundled clothing, waiting for their names to be called off again, and to be moved to where they would receive their convict uniform. Watching them was a young Coloured guard in a washed-out uniform and a big topi that looked ridiculous above his small face. He kept his face stern, assuming an air of authority against the grins and exchanged looks of the prisoners.

A guard came up the steps through the archway into the hall. He was short and had the chest and shoulders of a young bear, and the thick, bowed legs of an ape in the khaki trousers. His blonde hair was cropped short, and he had a round face with knobbly cheek-bones, a puckered mouth that was merely a pink orifice, and little blue eyes, flat as pieces of glass under his blonde brows.

His complexion, normally pink, was flushed red with anger and impatience, and coming through the archway, finding that the crowd had overflowed across the thoroughfare, he hurled himself suddenly at them, shouldering the men into a stumbling, clawing rout against the wall.

"– – – – off," he shouted furiously. "You think this is a – – – – bar-room?"

He stood, short and squat and menacing, in the showy hall with its dusty Victorian cornicing and shabby grey walls. The blue eyes glared around at the crowded prisoners, and then he looked away from them towards the counter.

"Listen," he said. "How long must I wait to check these bastards' property?"

The warder who was taking thumb-prints said, "We're almost finished. But Meulen has got to write out the cards still."

"I'm going as fast as I can, mate," another clerk said. He was at a table behind the counter, writing out small cards from the forms passed to him. These cards showed the name, number and offence of each prisoner.

"Well, I've got to go off duty," the short guard said. "Jesus, must a man waste his time on these – – – –?" He glared around again. The prisoners were all silent, sensing the menace that came from him.

He shouted again, for no apparent reason, "You think this is a blerry hotel? This is a jail, *jong*. Here you will shit." Then he turned away and stalked out of sight down the steps to the lower room.

The other guards, spurred on by the short one's anger, began to hurry things up. Names were shouted, and men sprang forward, bumping each other to be in time. The man writing the ID cards at the table was shouting each name and flinging the card away without lifting his face, as he wrote the next card, so that the prisoners had to scramble for them.

"Abraham Hendricks .... William Johnson, housebreak .... Dammit, these names .... Joseph Collins .... Peterson, Aubrey .... Sam Baatjes, rape, hey?"

The naked convicts were all being herded away by the Coloured warder to where their uniforms waited in a big sack: canvas or corduroy shorts and faded red shirts.

The man taking prints was still yelling names as if he was competing with the one who wrote out the cards. Beyond the barred windows in the wall behind the counter, the sunlight was beginning to fade.

The warder writing the cards called, "George Adams," and then hesitated to look at what he had written. Then he looked up again as George Adams stepped forward.

"Another – – – – Communist," the man at the table said. "What, are you a kaffir? This – – – – jail is getting full of – – – – Communists." Then he grinned, a grimace that split his hard face like the mark made by an axe-blade. He turned to the one taking the thumb-prints and said, "Look here, *ou kerel*. Look at this. You reckon he'll get to be Prime Minister?"

The other looked around and sneered while he took a print. "Hell, not *him*. He's too bloody small."

The one at the table laughed and flung the card at George Adams who caught it deftly in mid-air. He turned away, thinking angrily, – – – – you, and the man at the table was already calling, "Albert March, murder...."

George Adams moved over to join the others who had already gone through the finger-printing and the issue of ID cards. He looked at his own card. It said: – – – – *Gaol. Awaiting Trial.* Then a number and his name and the date, and *Charge: Illegal organisation.* He thrust the card into the top pocket of his coat, and then found Jefferson waiting with the rest of the prisoners.

Jefferson said, "You got your card? Listen, look after it. Anywhere you go in this place you got to have that card with you. You lose it and these Dutchmen give you the works." He added, grinning: "It's like a pass, hey."

George Adams said, "If these buggers get funny, I'm going to kick up a noise. You'll see." He reached under his jacket and scratched his armpit. He needed a bath, and his beard felt like emery-paper.

A prisoner looked at him and said, "You men political?"

"*Ja*," George Adams told him.

"– – – – govvermen'. Some of your pals was released on bail yesterday."

"Yes? How many?"

"Don't know for sure, pally. But none of this papa's people." He jerked a thumb in the direction of Jefferson.

George Adams told him, "Well, I'm remanded for a month. No bail."

"– – – – guvvermen'," the other man whispered. "We got to have a – – – – revverlution."

After that they had to go down and have their property checked in the lower room. The property bags came up from the police-station and the prison went through them with each newcomer. Everybody walked down and lined up in front of another counter at which sat the short, angry warder, attended by a convict.

Here they started calling names all over again. The convict droned out the contents of the bags while the warder checked them against the receipt. Anything a remand prisoner was entitled to keep was handed back to him. George Adams was given his razor and a half-empty packet of cigarettes, and was told that he had fifty-eight cents in cash on the books.

He stepped back into line, examining the razor. He had a towel, but the packet of razor-blades, which his landlady had sent him at the police-station, they had kept, and he wondered now whether he should grow a beard. Going back to the line, he bumped into somebody and looked up, saying: "Sorry, mate."

He shuffled into the place next to this prisoner, and George Adams saw a young, boyish face with soft, almost plump cheeks, beardless as a babe's, and a bitter mouth. Looking into the eyes, he saw that they were hard and grey and cold as pebbles on a beach when the tide goes out, and that they did not smile. The boy had cropped hair over a small round head, and a yellowish complexion, the colour of an old, gnawed bone.

George Adams said, making whispered conversation: "How you, pally?"

"Okay," the boy said grittily. The stony grey eyes did not look at him.

"What you here for, mate?"

"Murder," the boy said, almost absent-mindedly.

And George Adams thought, Jesus, *this* lighty. Murder? The boy's nonchalance awed him.

25

Then the warder at the counter was calling, "Albert March" and the boy was stepping away. He did not return to the place beside George Adams, but moved in somewhere else in the lines.

George Adams whispered to Jefferson who stood on the other side of him: "Such a youngster, and murder." Then he added, frowning, "Well, maybe it's just a mistake. He might not be the bloke." He stood there, thinking about it, until guards were shouting again, separating Coloured from Africans, and Jefferson was saying, "See-you-sometime-George," brushing past him with a wink and a grin, and was gone.

After that the rest of them were assembled in twos, and under the eyes of a guard, were told sharply to "Step out."

They shuffled from the hall, up through the archway and across the hall where clerks and trusties worked, on, out into the yard again. The sunlight had disappeared from the surrounding stonework, but it clung to the slab of sky overhead, seeming to mock them, and they marched down the yard, past a ramp where a Coloured guard stood rigidly at ease, staring ahead like the figure-head of a sailing-ship; to where another guard unlocked a steel-barred gate and through into another square, deserted now in the late afternoon, surrounded by a row of ground-floor cells with iron doors and judas-holes with iron flaps over them like patches over the single eyes of ranked Cyclopses, and the double-storeyed back walls of cell-blocks. Across this square to where a guard with an iron key unlocked yet another barred grille that led through a narrow tunnel under a square arch between two blocks; into a second square flanked by the headquarters and the kitchens, a wall and archway to the sick-bay section, and the high grille-work which sealed off the Awaiting-trial Sections, one for Coloureds, another for whites.

Patches of imprisoned sunlight lay on the asphalt floor of the square, with wide triangles and rectangles of grey shadow, all forming a futuristic design in two colours.

The prison cat, fat and sleek under its tortoise-shell fur, slunk across the square and disappeared down the alley to the kitchen.

The escort cried, "Okay, strip." Some of the men had already started removing their clothes, and the rest followed. The guard watched them, slapping his thigh with the strap of his truncheon.

While they undressed, another guard came down the iron staircase inside the section yard, from the cells upstairs. He crossed the yard, looking at his wrist-watch, and then produced his key and unlocked the grille that divided the yard from the square.

"Bath, bath," he snapped, and then said to the escort: "Bloody late today, *ou* mate."

"Another big lot of – – – – skollies," the escort sneered.

George Adams had removed his trousers and jacket, and was unbuttoning his shirt. Those ahead of him, already undressed, were dashing through the gate, stark naked, leaving behind bundles of clothing which the guard had searched, handling each garment gingerly, like a scientist working with highly dangerous bacteria. But before he could follow the men towards the showers, the guard who was looking at his wrist-watch again, was saying: "Hold on, you boggers."

The guard said to the escort: "Jussus, man, I am not going to wait. Going off now, *jong*. These bastards can wash in the morning, to hell with it. I'm not working blerry overtime."

The escort shrugged and the guard motioned George Adams and the others who still waited, into the yard. "Come on, jump, jump. Hurry up."

They gathered up their bundles of clothes, the naked ones from the showers hopping and skipping to dry themselves, and entered the yard. The two guards, one of them unlocking doors down the row, began allocating prisoners to cells.

George Adams went down the line, feeling the floor of

27

the yard warm through his socks. He had pulled on his trousers again, and was carrying his jacket and shoes. And when the guard's hand pushed him into a cell, he saw four men seated on their bedding, scratching themselves and staring at him.

The cell door thumped shut behind him and the lock grated and squeaked, and one of the men frowned at him and said, "They let you keep your kit, pally?"

George Adams grinned at him and said, "*Ja*, mate," telling himself that he had not got his bath after all.

3

Back in the Reception Hall, a uniformed clerk rose from his desk and came around the counter, waving a sheaf of papers, saying, "Now, where's those further charges?"

"They're around here," another man said, and jerked a thumb at a room off the main office. "Awaiting trial for attacking a warder."

The clerk went up to the door and snapped, "Come out, you."

The three men, barefooted and wearing the canvas jackets, red shirts and shorts of the Prisons Department, shuffled out of the room and stood in a line against a wall. The clerk checked their names from their ID cards against the papers in his hand, then went back to his desk. He signed a receipt and gave it to the guard who had escorted these men from another prison. They had been brought from that prison to the city jail where they were to await trial.

They stood quietly, with the blank faces of convicts who already knew the ropes, apparently seeing nothing, but all the time as alert as electric-meters, ready to move at a flick. One of these men had a knife-scar down the left side of his face from eyebrow to chin, and it gave him a lopsided look, as if his face had been hastily stuffed and sewn up. All had shaven heads and their mouths were still and sullen.

Earlier they had stood in the doorway of the room and had watched the new arrivals being checked in, and only when the little man, John Solomons, had skipped and pirouetted like a clown when his name had been called, had two of the convicts laughed aloud. Solly had turned and glared with simulated disgust at them, and had cried, "Whatter you boggers laughing for?" before a guard had yelled at him and he had skipped away. The scarface man had smiled, a toothy grimace.

Now they waited in line, until a guard snapped at them again to follow him, and they walked off quickly in single file. They went through the gates and the quiet yards, and then were marched into the square where the Isolation Block faced the Remand Section.

4

In the ceiling of the big cell a bulb behind a thick panel of glass sprayed a pale, diluted yellow light that did not reach the farthest corners. High up one wall the two barred windows were screened with dusty wire mesh which kept out all the twilight that was turning the sky lavender. On the floor, on rumpled blankets, sprawled or squatted most of the forty-odd inhabitants of the cell, while the remainder lounged about.

It seemed as if the heat of the day had been trapped in the cell with the prisoners, and it was packed in with them like a sort of invisible cotton wool, damp and sticky, aggravating the smell of breath and bodies. The fact that awaiting-trial prisoners were deprived of their outer clothing and shoes each time they were locked up for the night, did not make much difference. Naked or half-naked bodies only allowed the stench of sweat and unwashed blankets to circulate more freely with the other smells. Smells and heat were solid, enveloping, engulfing, as was the babble of sound in the caserne.

Different men bawling different songs, others talking aloud to make themselves heard above the singing, still others arguing and creating an uproar simply for the sake of creating an uproar, all contributed to the general pandemonium.

Here and there parties crouched over games of tattered packs of handmade or smuggled cards, draughts played with scraps of paper or chips of coal for counters on boards scratched out on the floor, or shot dice for each other's clothing. This was the ground-floor main cell. On the upper floor was another, where the bedlam was twice as bad.

Pandemonium would abdicate for a while when the night-guard reached the cell on his rounds around the section, and shouted through the peep-hole in the iron door.

Butcherboy Williams was asking, "What you baskets in here for?" He had herded a group of newcomers into a corner and was glowering at them with his blood-flecked eyes.

Gang leader, and incidentally cell boss by virtue of his brutality and the backing of bullied and equally vicious toadies, he was mean as a jackal, blood-thirsty as a wolf, foul as a hyena, and the group whom he had trapped in the corner shuffled nervously on their feet, and avoided the palaeoanthropic glare.

Only the man called Solly showed no sign of nervousness. He screwed up a wrinkled face and laughed, the sound springing from his gullet with the stridency of a rooster.

"*Dronk* and disor'erly, *ou man*," he cried, cackling.

"Dronk and disor'erly, *mos, ou* pal."

"You," sneered Butcherboy, "I know you, *ou* Solly. Drunk, *ja*. But disor'erly, never. What in hell can *you* do what's disor'erly? *Gwan*."

"Me, reckon and think," Solly cackled. And he danced like a marionette, a grotesque jig in front of the savage hulk. He was a smudged and tattered, crumpled memo-sized, yellow duplicate of a man, with eyes like smeared plus-signs in the wrinkle folds of his face, a mouth like a blurred dash flanked by deep-cut parentheses. His hard skull was covered with full stops of peppercorn hair and his forehead scored with myriad lines. His scrawny miniature body was clad in a stained and filthy shirt, several sizes too large for it, that reached down to the scurf-covered joints of his knees.

He danced up and down, grinning up at Butcherboy with his toothless mouth and clapped together his gnarled hands. "Hey, Butcherboy," he crowed. "Reckon and think, *ou* pal."

"Gwan," Butcherboy growled again. He was half-naked, revealing an ape-like torso covered with tattooed decorations: hands holding hands, a skull-and-crossbones, a Union Jack, a dripping dagger, and various other emblems consistent with his barbarism. Below his waist he wore a pair of old khaki shorts over full-length and filthy pyjama pants, giving him a ludicrous appearance in spite of the powerful brutality.

Now he towered over the little man, massive hands on his waist, and grinned with sinister humour. *"Gwan,* man," he said croakily. "You couldn't hurt a baby, you."

"Listen," Solly cackled, shuffling in another version of his original dance. "Reckon and think, pally. Listen, man."

The others, relieved by this diversion, started to sidle cautiously away, while the attention of Butcherboy was being distracted.

"Hear me," Solly was telling Butcherboy. "Reckon and think. There is I in that canteen. The Wellington Arms, *mos.* You know *mos* that place, don't I say? Awright, there I is. Reckon and think, I'm having a small white at the bar when this *juba* come in."

"What *juba*?" scowled Butcherboy.

"Wait, man. Listen. I'm telling you, *mos.* This rooker come in come up to the bar, and he is just like this: 'Gimme a banana lick-your.' Well, I look at him, and I reckon: 'Banana lick-your? Banana blerry lick-your? What you reckon this is, pal? The blerry Gran' Hotel? *Banana* lick-your. That's *mos* a blerry woman's drink.' This rooker look at me and say: 'Min' your own business.' And, 'Oh,' I say.

31

'Blerry highty-tighty, hey?' 'Go to hell,' this rooker reckon. 'You's drunk.' Well, I'm getting damn fed up with his blerry highty-tighty ways, see. So I reckon to him: 'Oh, so a man can't get drunk, hey? Man can't have a blerry dop without you highty-tighty baskets putting your nose in, hey? Banana lick-your. I'll give you – – – – banana lick-your.' And I just grab him, and then –"

His narration was drowned by a sudden uproar from another part of the cell, and Butcherboy turned his neolithic head and bellowed, "Shut your – – – – ing mouths, you sonamabitches." When the noise had subsided to a mutter, he turned again to the little man and growled: "Go on."

"Awright," Solly cackled. "Like I was saying, I grab this *juba* and reckon: 'Okay, you think you *mos* big and you talk big also, hey?' And the barman reckon to me: 'Hey, stop that.' And I reckon back to him: 'Ah, – – – – you, too, man.' And this john I'm holding give me a clout when I'm not looking and I turn and tell him: 'Oh, you hard case. Awright, *ou* pally. You'll see.' So I give him like this, quick."

And before Butcherboy could ward him off, the little man grasped him by the shoulders and the miniature body shot upwards, the hard skull butting, driving like a shell from a cannon.

Butcherboy cried, "Hey!" and jerked his face aside in the nick of time, pushing the little man off, growling.

"Awright, man," Solly crowed, his wrinkled face squirming with laughter. "I was only showing you."

"Don't get funny," Butcherboy said. "Go on."

"Awright. Well, that spoil his nice jacket, see? And then we's all over the – – – – ing bar, in among the tables and the rest of the crowd, and drinks is spilling all over the place, and me giving this *juba* the head. Look –" He bowed his head and pointed out several lumps and abrasions with a dirty finger that looked remarkably like a withered twig. Then he went on.

"This rooker give a couple with the knee, and I reckon: 'Oh, using your feet, hey. I'll show you.' I give him a few more with the head, and his – – – – nose and mouth is bleeding and he got a thick eye. But the blerry barman, he phone the law in the meantime, the coward, and on top of that he and a couple of other rookers, they get hold of me and stop the fight.

"Well, I don't want to cause a disturbance, *mos,* so I keep still and wait until the law come. I didn't *mos* do nothing wrong, don't I say? Only this *juba* with his – – – – banana lick-your. Banana lick-your, I ask you."

"What happen when you came in front?" Butcherboy asked. "Is only two poun' or ten days, I think."

"*Garn.* I plead not guilty, man."

"Not guilty? You crazy," Butcherboy sneered. "You reckon you going to get off? You could have started the ten days awready."

Solly looked sly, and broke into a cackle, dancing his crazy jig again. "Well, I got my reasons, reckon and think," he said.

Butcherboy looked at him suspiciously, and then said, *"Gwan."* After that he turned his back, broad as a door, on the little man and looked around the cell. He started to kick his way through the tangle of bodies on the floor, bawling, "Where's those other new baskets what just come in? I want to see those – – – – baskets, hey."

He reached his bed: by confiscating the blankets of several of his fellows he had built himself a mattress which considerably relieved the discomfort of the concrete floor, and a few more blankets had gone into the making of a pillow. Now he straddled the bed and stared menacingly around the caserne, while his obsequious retinue, including Brakes Peterson, Pinks, Moos and Squinteye Samuels, flanked him, all demonstrating their allegiance with admiring grins, which however, on closer scrutiny, would have revealed certain elements of hatred and mockery.

The great man flexed his muscles and swelled the tattooed torso so that the pictures writhed like animated cartoons. He slapped his massive chest and biceps with hands like the grabs of a dredger. The small, bright eyes leaped around like sparks.

"Let me see," he rumbled. "There's some baskets here I don't know, yet."

The eyes continued to peer from face to face and fixed upon a man with a pock-marked chin and face as evil as a vulture, who lounged gloomily nearby.

"*Jy*, you. Come here, man. Jump, jump."

The man did not move.

"Jump, you basket," Butcherboy hissed.

The man looked at his shoe-button eyes, gathered saliva in his mouth and spat.

"Bring him to me," snarled Butcherboy, and in a second the newcomer had been seized by neck, seat of trousers, and rushed towards the waiting cell boss. A fist like a mallet struck, and the face exploded into a spray of blood.

The man sagged in the grip of his captors and Butcherboy seized him by his waist-band, and as the others released the man, lifted him high and then flung him carelessly across the cell. Prisoners scattered and the man's body struck the wall and slid to the floor where he lay, making sounds like a hurt animal.

Butcherboy laughed hoarsely, and his henchmen chuckled. His tiny eyes now caught sight of a slight-looking, but wire-tough youth who had the young-old face of a slum child. "Who's this lighty?" he asked, speaking with the hoarse voice which went with damaged vocal chords.

"They call him *mos* The Casbah Kid," answered Brakes Peterson, who had only one good side to his face. The other was a hideous mapwork of wrinkles and folds caused by a carelessly treated burn received when his mistress, tired of a life of brutality, had held a hot flat-iron to his cheek in revenge, one night when he lay asleep.

"They going to hang him, *mos*," Brakes laughed. "He's here for murder."

"Oh, a hard-case lighty. don't I say?" Butcherboy laughed grittily. "Come here, lighty."

The boy strolled forward and his eyes were dull and hard in the watery light of the bulb in the ceiling. He bit a thumb-nail, looked at it, and then looked at Butcherboy.

The big man's mouth moved, revealing broken teeth. "What's your name, lighty?"

"March. Albert March."

"What did you do, lighty?"

"Murder." The boy spoke as if homicide was a normal activity, like going to the latrine or scratching an itch.

"You talk big, lighty."

"I don't like to talk at all, man," the boy replied. He bit at another nail and examined it, ignoring Butcherboy's gaze.

"Hell, he's *mos* a smart lighty, too."

Wiping the finger on the side of his jeans, the boy muttered, "Some *jubas* like to talk, *mos. I* don't like to talk, man."

"Well, pally, when you talk with me, you talk like you talking to big folk, see?" And a hand swung out and slapped the boy away.

The Casbah Kid sprawled, but only for a second, then bounced to his feet like a ball, snarling. The next second he was launched like a projectile across the cell, head down and aimed directly at Butcherboy's stomach. Had he landed, his hard skull, propelled by one hundred and twenty pounds of weight, would have knocked the surprised Butcherboy doubled-up, winded, perhaps helpless. But the giant was ready and he did the right thing at the right moment.

He grunted and his knee jerked up and crashed into the mouth of the butting youth.

When The Casbah Kid came to, everybody had turned in, rolled in blankets or lying exposed in the heat. He dragged himself upright, spat out a tooth and fingered his broken lip. He did not have to consider whether or not he should take revenge for Butcherboy's assault. Vengeance slipped into his mind with the ease of the sprockets of an oiled wheel into the links of a greased chain.

He got up and went over to the water urn and washed the blood away, then drank a mouthful. He looked across to where Butcherboy's heavy form stirred with the effort of his brontosaurian snores, and then turned away to examine the rest of the cell.

Walking silently, he crossed over sleeping bodies, peering around, and then discovered an old pilchard can which was used as an ashtray by somebody. He crouched and began to unwind the long key from the curled tin.

When he had the key free, the boy stepped over to a vacant space against the wall and sat down. He began to rub the straight end of the key carefully against the concrete of the floor between his feet, working quietly, wearing the metal down to a point, stopping only when somebody stirred or tossed in his sleep, and then continuing again, to hone the key into a sharp spike.

5

Three of the men in the cell had been interrupted in their game of rummy played with a pack of greasy cards which they had stuffed into hiding under the blankets when the door had been unlocked.

They were a nondescript trio, wearing a grimy miscellany of shorts, singlets and unwashed shirts, crouching together under the insipid bulb in the ceiling. When the door was re-locked, they drew the cards from under the rumpled blankets and, having given George Adams a greeting of careless nods, returned to the game, studying intently their respective hands.

The cell was cramped and hot, and in one corner next to the door stood the night-soil bucket, and in the other, the water urn. The barred window high up the rear wall was covered with grime, and four metal mugs hung from a length of bent wire attached to the screen.

George Adams was looking around for a place where he could settle down, when the fourth man spoke. He was the one who had asked George Adams about his clothes.

"Make yourself by the house, pal." He had a casual voice, full of a sort of mocking humour. And he thrust out a foot and nudged one of the others in the back, saying, "Move over, mate. Give this john some place."

The three others squirmed about on the spread blankets, without taking their eyes off their cards, and left a section where George Adams could stretch out. He said, "Thanks, men," but they took no notice of him, so he smiled at the other man.

George Adams placed his shoes against the wall and folded his coat over them, then he sat down and stretched his legs. He felt sticky, and the heat of the cell seemed to bank up in layers. Somewhere, in another cell voices were singing *Gallway Bay* and from another part of the prison came the clang of a footstep on an iron stair.

"Well, mate," the fourth man said, "Here we are, broken-hearted, hey."

George Adams smiled at him and he grinned back. He asked, "Didn't they give you no blankets?"

"We got in late," George Adams answered. "I reckon the warder didn't want to open up the store."

"Those baskets don't move their backsides unless they really got to. Hear me, mate. When they open up and we had breakfast tomorrow morning, you ask the section warder for blankets and a mug. You don't ask, they don't care, understand?"

"I'll do that," George Adams said. He felt a little relieved at meeting somebody ready to be friendly.

In this half-world, hemmed in by stone and iron, there was an atmosphere of every-man-for-himself which George Adams did not like. He had grown up in the slums and he knew that here were the treacherous and the wily, the cringers and the boot-lickers, the violent and the domineering, the smooth-talkers and the savage, the bewildered and the helpless; the strong preyed on the weak, and the strong and brutal acknowledged a sort of nebulous alliance among themselves for the terrorisation of the underlings.

George Adams was thinking about it when the fourth man broke into his thoughts.

"First time in, *ou* mate?"

"*Ja*. Oh, I've been locked up in police-stations, but this is the first time that I come here."

George Adams looked at this man. He was thin and lean, lounging angularly in his corner, like a discarded folding-ruler, and he had a lean, smooth, handsome face, tan-coloured, with white dentures flashing in it when he smiled. Like others, he had contrived to hang on to his clothes, and his shirt was a flamboyant green, his pegged trousers neat and clean, as if, even here, he took pains to maintain his flashiness. This was the gentleman gangster, a member of the underworld aristocracy – not the street-corner lounger, but a frequenter of the upstairs billiard rooms along Hanover and Caledon Streets, where plots were hatched against a background of clacking cues and drifting smoke.

He lounged in his corner, as far from the ammoniac smell of the latrine bucket as he could get, long and lean and sleek and bright and dangerous as a knife-blade.

He asked the inevitable question with affability: "What you in for, mate?"

George Adams was feeling hot and the perspiration spotted his brow, and he unbuttoned his shirt, to slip it off, as he said, "Political. Working against the government."

The three paused in their silent game of cards to look at him with curiosity, and the other man broke into a chuckle. He said, nodding slowly, "Ah, the Resistance. Read about it." He sat up and went on with bright-eyed enthusiasm. "The sabotage men, *mos*. Don't I say? There was some johns over on the other side what they blew some railway property, I think. Hell, mate, that's big business, hey?"

George Adams said carefully, slipping out of his trousers so that now he was in vest and shorts, "Just organising and things, man."

He wiped moisture from his face with a finger. The other three had turned back to their cards. He rummaged through his coat until he found a crumpled cigarette packet. It contained four slightly bent cigarettes and he straightened the packet, offering it to the lean man, but the latter shook his head, saying: "You smoke, pally. I got some."

The man winked. "My goose keep me well supplied, hey." Then, when George Adams took out a cigarette and offered it to one of the card-players, he asked, scowling: "Hell, what for you giving tobacco away? These baskets can find their own, *mos*, don't I say?"

"Hell," George Adams told him, "We all in this – – – – together."

The card-player took the cigarette and smiled at George Adams, who said, "You men got to share it, I reckon."

"Is okay, mister," another player said and saluted with a finger to his forehead.

The lean man produced a lighter and snapped the flame and held it to George Adams's cigarette. As far as he was concerned Adams was an equal, an expert from the upper echelons of crime, but generosity came hard to him as he offered the lighter with reluctance to the card-player. When he had put the lighter away, he said, "Oh, yes, mate. My name is Yusef Ebrahim. My pallies, they call me Yusef the Turk, likely."

George Adams introduced himself, smiling at the other through the smoke that was now beginning to drift in the cell, and asked, "And what they take you for, mate?"

Yusef the Turk laughed gently, and then scowled suddenly, sitting up straight and looking at George Adams. "*Garn*, it was hell of a crack charge, man." He shook his sleek, shiny head. "They say *mos* I he'ped to rob a facktry. *Ghod*, these law, they take a man for any blerry thing, don't I say?"

"I reckon it happens," George Adams said. The smoke drifted around them, but nobody paid attention to it, but the heat clung on and the smoke made the air thick as flannel.

The lean man pointed a finger at him, and jabbed the air as he spoke. "Look mate, you's *mos* a man with understanding. Don't I say? I reckon you know something of the law, *mos*. You studied the govvermen'."

"Hell, I don't know so good," George Adams smiled.

"Awright," said Yusef the Turk. "Look at it like this, mate. I'm standing outside this facktry in Salt River, hey. Maybe strolling up and down a little. I'm just there doing likely nothing, see. There's nobody about, see. Just a car nearby, parked likely. I'm not doing nothing. Just standing about, like, and minding my own blerry business. Doing nothing. Then some johns come running out of the facktry gate carrying a sort of bag between them."

He paused and scratched under his shirt, withdrew the hand and looked at what he had caught, and then crushed it against the wall. One of the card-players rose and went to the latrine bucket.

"Awright," Yusef the Turk continued. "So these johns come running out of the facktry, like, with the sack. The next thing, the Flying Squad come round the corner, taking it on two wheels, so fast they come. Well, look here, man. These two johns, they drop the sack and the next thing they are running like hell, scraping up the street . . . ."

From outside came the clang of a barred gate and the drag of booted feet across the concrete floor of the yard. The lean man motioned to George Adams to kill the cigarette, and the card-players again hid their cards, stretching out as if ready to sleep.

The footsteps of the night-guard and the sound of his cough echoed in the yard as he moved from door to door. Then the flap of the peep-hole into their cell was lifted and George Adams saw the guard's eye peering in at them. Then the eye was gone and the hole covered again. They listened to the footsteps moving and stopping, then moving again, around the yard and then up the iron staircase to the gallery above.

One of the card-players said, "Is almost ducking time. I'm not playing no more."

"Okay, then," another agreed. "We can turn in."

Yusef the Turk was saying, ". . . . always watching and peeping, like." Then he returned to his story. "Like I was saying, there's these johns scraping up the street, and I'm standing there, knowing about nothing, hey. And what you reckon these law do?" The lean finger jabbed the air towards George Adams. "They stop their car and get out, and they grab *me*." He snorted. "How you like that? What did I do? I was just standing there, *mos*."

George Adams shrugged and said, "Well, you got to tell it to your lawyer."

"Lawyer, his mother," Yusef the Turk said sourly. "Just out to make money. Me, I can talk for myself. *Ya Allah*, there I am, standing outside this facktry, doing nothing, and now I's here, for housebreak and thef'." He shook his head and got up and went over to the water urn, taking a mug with him. "You reckon that's right?" he asked. "You reckon that's right?"

"Those law turn up pretty quick, man," George Adams said.

Yusef the Turk emptied his mug and returned to his corner, then grinned at George Adams, stretching himself out on his blankets.

"Well, it happen that we didn't tie the watchman up so good when we get into the facktry. So he get loose and phone the Squad. Well, there's the last bell. We got to turn in now."

6

The rear bumper of the old car was loose and clattered with the sound of metal against metal as they drove along, and George Adams, sitting beside Jefferson Mpolo who was driving, remembered vaguely the sounds of the machines in the factory where he had once worked. Jefferson drove steadily, carefully nursing the car along, his eyes intent on the stained wind-screen. Under his thighs, George Adams could feel the hardness of a bare spring where the upholstery had come apart. They drove through the quiet street, past lighted houses with high porches and garden walls, and street lamps which made puddles of yellow light on the sidewalks.

"Are we nearly there, George?" Jefferson asked.

"Just keep straight on," Adams told him. "We got to turn right. I'll tell you where."

Jefferson drove on. He belched and said, "We had fish for supper, man. I'm bladdy thirsty, guy."

"You think they'll have the stuff ready?" Adams asked. "We don't want to wait."

"They better have it ready. I want to get home early. Lena's got a cold."

"You get a doctor?"

"Nah. Just the 'flu. She will get better, man."

They went on along the road past the neat, wide, fairly new houses. Some of them had tall palms growing in the gardens, creepers, and stained-glass front doors. George Adams looked out and thought that here were the well-to-do of his community: the professionals, the clerks, the artisans, small-time businessmen and some of the border-liners who went through life sorry they had not been born a shade lighter so they could slip across and be white.

He said, with a grin, "Well, the cops don't prowl around here much."

"Real classy folks, hey," Jefferson said.

"Government will declare this area white, you'll see," Adams said. "Then the poor baskets will have to go." He stared ahead through the yellowed wind-screen, and spoke again. "Second turning on the right, Jeff. By that house with the high stoop."

They clattered around the corner into another street, and George Adams said, "Talk about security. This bus is enough to wake the dead."

"Hey, man," Jefferson laughed. "This is the Rolls Royce of the location. I'm a bladdy capitalis'."

"Who knows?" Adams laughed. "You better stop here," he said. "We'll walk up."

The old car clamoured to a stop, and the engine coughed wrackingly and then became silent. Adams opened the door on his side carefully, because the hinges were faulty, and he did not step on the old-fashioned running-board because it was as treacherous as a man-trap. He slammed the door to make it hold, then stood on the kerb-side, waiting for Jefferson.

The night was warm, but there was a slight breeze blowing here in this district near the mountainside. Looking downhill, he could see the lights of the city and the docks with the masts of ships like antennae against the sea. Over the city the neon lights glowed behind a haze, looking as if the rooftops were burning.

"Okay, guy, let's go," Jefferson said.

"It's down this way," Adams said, and they went off along the street.

They passed a row of houses behind low walls, the sounds of voices and laughter coming from beyond glowing curtains, and crossed an intersection, strolling through the electric lozenges of light from the street lamps. Jefferson was whistling *Tuxedo Junction* under his breath, and George Adams lighted a cigarette and spun the match away into the gloom.

They came up to a row of darkened shops: a grocery store, a barber's, a pharmacy, and then George Adams touched Jefferson's arm and said as they stopped outside a butcher shop, "Here we are, man."

The front of the butchery was in darkness. The tiled display shelf in the window was bare, but the pane was still covered with price lists painted in white window-cleaner. George Adams looked up and down the street to make sure that it was clear, then started to rap on the glass door of the shop.

Jefferson asked in a whisper, "This shop belong to one of our people?"

"Just a sympathiser," Adams told him. "Gives donations now and then."

Somewhere a hooter sounded. Jefferson belched again and left the faint aroma of fish on the bight air, while George Adams rapped once more on the plate glass of the door.

This time there was the sound of unlocking and the door was opened an inch.

"It's me, George," Adams said into the crack. "I got Jeff with me."

"Oh. Okay, George-boy."

The door was pulled open and the two entered the darkened shop. There was a smell of slaughtered meat in the air inside the butchery, mingled with that of sawdust and disinfectant. From a room at the back came the clicking sound of a machine.

George Adams led the way across the shop. A big refrigerating vault took up most of the back wall, and there was a counter with a scale and a cash register on it, standing in the gloom.

The man who had let them in was saying: "How you, Jeff? Long time no see, man."

"Been busy," Jefferson told him. "You chaps got the leaflets finish yet?"

George Adams opened the door at the back of the shop and they went into the small, lighted room which had painted-over windows and sawdust on the floor. A row of butcher-knives and cleavers hung against one wall, over a sausage-making machine. There was a sink and other things associated with a butchery, all over the place. The duplicating machine had been set up next to a table piled with stacks of finished leaflets. The machine was running and a girl, with a smudge of ink on her chin, and reddish hair was watching it.

"Hul-lo George, hul-lo Jeff," she said, looking up at them. "Hell, Jeff, I haven't seen you in a helluva time." She smiled at them.

Jefferson said admonishingly, "You didn't turn up to that meeting last week."

"I couldn't make it. Really I couldn't." She gathered up printed sheets and stacked them. "You're not mad, are you?"

"I'll let you off this time," Jefferson smiled. He went over to the sink and drank from the tap. Wiping his mouth, he asked, "Our stuff ready?"

"We just got to tie them up," the man who had let them in, said. He was young and stout, his new paunch bulging over his belt, and he had a hooked nose and pock-marked cheeks.

George Adams looked at him, poking the belly playfully. "Jesus, Cassim, you getting fat."

"Isn't he?" the girl laughed. "I was telling him he should go on diet."

"I'm not giving up four meals a day for anybody," Cassim laughed. He said, "Well, let's tie up this stuff, then you buggers can push off."

The three of them gathered around the table and began to work at the stacks of papers. Adams picked up a leaflet and looked at it. "Didn't come out too bad," he said.

"Considering that this bloody machine conks in every five minutes," the girl said.

Cassim laughed, making a parcel of a pile of leaflets, "I see that big wall down in New Market Street was painted all over with slogans."

Jefferson said in mock surprise, "Yeah? I wonder who could of done it. Messing up people's walls."

They made several parcels and then George Adams said, "Reckon that's the lot. Six thousand. We got to deliver them still."

The girl said, "Lucky blighters. Here I've got to stand over this bloody machine till God knows when."

Cassim laughed again, saying, "Well, you're the expert, *mos*. Who told you to become an office worker?"

She stuck her tongue out at him and wiped her inky hands on a piece of waste. "Go away and leave me alone, Cas."

Adams said to Jefferson, "You go around and bring the bus, Jeff. We'll wait by the door for you."

They picked up bundles of leaflets and went out into the front of the shop after Jefferson. The girl came to the door of the room and said: "Good luck, boys."

Cassim put down his leaflets and unlocked the door, and Jefferson went out. Adams said, "Nice of this guy to let us use his place."

"Damn," Cassim laughed. "He was scared as hell. But I talked him into it, anyway."

The girl had shut the back-room door, and they stood there in the dark. Adams could hear the fat youth's heavy breathing as they waited, and then they heard the rattle of the car coming down the street, and its shrill wheezing as it pulled up outside.

Later they were driving away from that part of the city, clattering downhill, the old car puttering and jolting. The breeze from behind the mountain had strengthened and it l aned against the loose-jointed sides of the car.

"Wind coming up," George Adams said, sitting in the corner beside Jefferson Mpolo. "Might blow like hell tomorrow."

Jefferson said, "Yeah, boy. Listen, your people organised okay for tonight?"

"I reckon so. You got to take a chance with what you got," Adams said. "People volunteer, so you got to accep' them. Lot of people got the jitters nowadays. 'Fraid of the cops."

"I hope nothing goes wrong, man."

"Why? You worried about your side?"

"No, man. But a good few of these people we don't know well. Like you said, we got to take a chance with them."

They rolled into the slum quarter of the city, past rows of dark stores: furniture, groceries, delicatessen, a barred and empty cinema with the wind worrying the billboards, and scarred and broken walls on which the exposed brickwork showed like scabless sores.

Adams lighted a cigarette and thought of the bundles of

illegal leaflets on the back seat of the car. He was a little apprehensive about them, and wished that they had done with the delivery, that the bundles were out of their hands and that they could both go home. He was not scared, he told himself, but you always felt this way when you had to travel distances with this kind of thing.

He said to Jefferson, "Turn here." The other belched again and eased his foot on the accelerator, twisting the wheel and they turned down a long dark street where scraps of papers were being blown about by the wind, dancing like elfin ghosts across the mottled black-grey asphalt.

Jefferson pulled up at the kerb at Adam's instructions, and a man came out of an alleyway. He stepped into the yellow light of the headlamps and came round to where Adams sat, touching his shabby hat and smiling. He had a ragged grey moustache, like unravelling wool.

"Evening, George," he said "Howsit? We're waiting for you."

George Adams leaned over the seat and picked up two parcels, passing them to the man, through the window.

"Hullo, Mister Peters. Sorry to keep you up this time of night."

"Is okay, Georgie. Is okay. You awright?"

"Fine. You know what to do, hey, Mister Peters?"

"Yessir. You leave it to us. I got my three boys ready to go, and two others."

"Good. Well, we got to be on our way."

"That's okay. Goo' night."

They drove off towards the main road and out of the city into the suburbs. It was long past midnight when they had delivered most of the parcels, and now, going down a tree-lined road through an undeveloped area, George Adams said, "Well, two more bundles, and we can go home."

"One of my contacts should be waiting near the end of this road," Jefferson said. "I hope the bladdy buggah turn up."

"You reckon he might change his mind?"

"Fairly new guy," Jefferson said. "Did a couple of things, and he looks willing enough."

"I hope none of these chaps throw the bloddy stuff down the first drain they pass, that's all," Adams said.

Jefferson slowed down and peered ahead. Over them the sky was dark and blue, an old spread of serge scattered with imitation diamonds, and the wind was stiff in the open country, moving the tops of the trees so that they swayed like a choir. Beyond the fields the darker ridge formed by a housing project made a ragged and smudgy barrier across the horizon.

"Somewhere around here," Jefferson said, braking the car. A dirt road made by a construction company cut into the main road from behind some trees.

"You reckon we ought to wait?" Adams asked.

And then headlights snapped on suddenly, merging with their own, breaking into the darkness around the dirt road, and they saw the outline of a big car behind the glare.

Jefferson asked, "Now what?" as another car swung out of the adjacent darkness and pulled up close and across the front of them and more lights washed over the old car.

Men were surrounding the car and they heard somebody laugh. They sat still as the faces of plain-clothes men peered in, and the doors were jerked open.

A man said, looking at them, "How, it's *ou* Adams and *ou* Jefferson." The voice was full of arrogant humour. "How you Jefferson? Man, you boys are riding *mos* around late. Going to meet some girls?"

Another man laughed, and a third said, "Come on, come on, let's see what they're up to."

"Out, *comrades*," the first man said, chuckling.

Adams and Jefferson climbed out into the sharp glare of the headlamps and flash-lights. George Adams kept his hands in the pockets of his jacket. He recognised some of the detectives of the Security Police. Jefferson stood by him, his broad dark face without expression in the harsh light. Two men were searching the inside of the old car.

The one who had spoken first, said, smiling: "You feeling okay, George?"

George Adams looked at this one, but said nothing. He was feeling angry and frustrated, and his hands clenched in his pockets.

Another man standing by sneered and said, "George-ovski. Why isn't your name George-ovski. You buggers should be in – – – – Russia. Not here."

The two who had been in the car now climbed back into the road, one of them carrying the bundles of leaflets in his arms. He said, "We found this. There's nothing else." He was speaking to a tall, broad, hefty man with a red face and a nose like an owl's, who was in charge of the party.

"We'll look at it at the station," this man said. He turned to the two who were standing with Jefferson and Adams. "You men ride with these. We'll follow."

The one who had been joking all the time motioned them back into the car, directing George Adams to the rear seat. They climbed in and the man who had spoken about Russia sat in the front with Jefferson. All the others had scattered to their respective cars, and the one in the dirt road roared into life, swinging out in front of Jefferson, to lead the way.

"Okay, Jeff, follow them," the detective beside him said.

The three cars moved off down the long, tree-lined road. Jefferson stared ahead, frowning a little. George Adams sat in the corner away from the detective with him. He was still angry, and his heart beat awkwardly.

The detective in front said, "You ought to get another car, Jeff. This one is almost falling to pieces."

"They ought to send to Russia for a car," the one in the back said.

Then the two of them laughed and the cars swept on along the road towards where the glow of electroliers made a purple haze along the suburban highway.

7

At five-thirty in the morning a guard stepped out of the Headquarters Block, opposite the Awaiting-trial Section, and began to hammer the iron triangle hanging from a sort of gallows in front of it.

It was just starting to grow light, and there was a wash of grey in the sky, gradually diluting the navy-blue and dissolving the stars. The breeze which had sprung up during the night died away like a ghost returning to the grave at dawn, and there was a promise of a clear day in the early air.

In the cells throughout the old prison there was a shuffling, cursing, pushing, shouting, grumbling; a general milling around as if an ant-heap had been disturbed. Blankets had to be folded and mats rolled up to clear the floor for sweeping. In the kitchen the cook's squad, who had turned up hours ago, were stacking tin bowls of breakfast onto high four-tiered trays: plain corn mush for Non-whites; mush with milk and sugar and slices of bread for the whites.

George Adams sat up and yawned, ran his hands over his face and wiped sleep from his eyes. His body was sore and stiff from sleeping on the hard mat. He had felt this way before, waking up in a police cell, so he took no particular notice of it, knowing that it would pass off as soon as his body became accustomed to the discomfort.

He stood up and pulled on his trousers and then his shoes, bending to lace them and feeling the twinge in his spine. He decided to leave his shirt off until he had washed.

The other men in the cell were folding their mats and blankets, yawning and stretching, eyes heavy with sleep. From beyond the cell came the various sounds of the waking prison.

"How you sleep, mate?" Yusef the Turk asked as he lighted a cigarette. He did not bother to fold his blankets, and when George Adams moved to help the other men who were doing it for him, he said: "How, let these *jubas* do it.

These small fry do all the things. They get a little something for it."

"Well, we're all in here together, man," George Adams told him. "Might as well share the work."

The lean man laughed and blew smoke. "Hell, pally, you got a lot to learn. You want to *mos* have an easy time in this blerry place. So you must learn to catch wire, man."

"I'll do my share," George Adams told him.

The other laughed again and slapped his back. "By Allah, you will learn, mate. You will learn. Hear me, the only johns who get by in this place is them what know how to get things done for them, them what is hard case enough to make others listen, and may be them that licks the guards' jack. Most of the time the lickers don't last long, anyway."

"I'm not aiming to lick anybody," George Adams said.

"That's it, that's it," Yusef the Turk grinned. "Never min', mate. Yussy will look after you, hey."

George Adams said sarcastically, "Awright, ma."

The others had rolled up the mats and lined them along the back wall of the cell, with the folded blankets on top of them. They sat in a row on the blankets, waiting for the door to be unlocked.

Yusef the Turk went over to the bucket, standing with his back towards George Adams, and said, "Hear me, when they finish giving our diet, you ask the section-guard for your mat and blankets, hey. You get two blankets."

"Right," George Adams said, sitting down by the three against the wall.

"Now this john in charge is a real hard-case basket," Yusef the Turk said. "You got to ask him nicely, like. He's a real basket, I'm telling you."

George Adams looked at him and frowned. "Nicely?" he asked. "What you mean, nicely? I got a right to have blankets, don't I say?"

"Rights," the lean man said, and he was not smiling. "Rights. You reckon you got rights, man? Listen, mate, only these – – – – warders got rights. *They* tell you what is rights."

51

"Well, there's regulations, *mos.*"

"Reggerlations? Naturally, there's reggerlations. But there's some reggerlations these baskets don't like, hey. You ask them something they don't like, and you see what happen." He laughed sourly. "You know how they work this jail? You can do as you blerry well please, only don't get in their way. You don't get in a guard's way and you's okay. Hear what I tell you, mate."

George Adams thought that he was probably right, but he was not going to give the impression that he would back down for anything. Once you showed you were scared or nervous about something, they were on you like wolves.

He said, casually, "Well, we see what happens, hey."

"You stay next to Yussy and things is going to go right," the other man said grinning.

George Adams lighted his last cigarette and sat there smoking. After a while he offered it to the man beside him, but the latter shook his head and smiled. "No, pally, you smoke. Is your last. We'll get others."

Yusef the Turk said, "I hope my goose send me some stuff today. That goose missed yesterday, she better watch out for herself. When you going to court?" he asked.

"Remanded for a month," George Adams answered. "No bail."

The other was about to say something else, but then the trample of boots sounded in the yard and doors were unlocked. They all got up as the big lock turned and the cell door thumped open. The guard yelled, "Out, out. Everybody out."

8

In the paling, dishwater-grey light in the section yard, the prisoners were milling around, most of them naked or half-naked, scrambling into their clothes while still others streamed down the iron staircase from the upper floor, carrying bundles and talking together, filling the yard with an incoherent rumbling and buzzing punctuated with the cries of the guards for everybody to form up.

The night shift, eager to go off duty, were helping the newly-arrived guards to line up the prisoners and start the count.

"Four-four, four-four," the guards were shouting as they poked with their drawn truncheons and slapped at bodies and heads with the straps on the handles. "Come on, you *bliksems*, fall in, fall in."

The prisoners moved over against a wall, dressing as they did so, scrabbling for lost shoes, clawing over the re-possession of filched articles of clothing, and gradually organising themselves into a column of fours, grumbling and cursing all the time.

"Fall in, fall in. Four-four, four-four," cried a voice as shrill as an overwound guitar-string. It was the little man, Solly, imitating the guards, leaping about as he pushed and pulled the men into line, his long ragged shirt, now worn over a pair of tattered shorts, whipping around so that he looked for all the world like a scarecrow come to life in the wind. "Fall in, fall in. Four-four."

One of the guards came up and slapped his back with a strap. "Go on, *donder*. You playing the fool? What you think this is, a circus?"

The little man laughed, his face puckered like a stale grenadilla, and skipped into the column, thrusting prisoners aside until he came up beside Butcherboy.

The huge man was leaning against the wall, his vast body slouched, ugly and brutal as a Neanderthal, the eyes savage as a wild boar's. He looked down at Solly and sneered, showing the irregular rows of stinking, carious teeth.

"What do you seek here, man?" he asked in a voice like a growl.

"*Ou* Butcherboy," cried the little man. "Morning, my pal. Look, mate, you got everything? Your shoes, your shirt?" He was wheedling, hoping to be admitted into the giant's circle while in prison. "I can cloak a shirt off one of these johns, *ou* pal, *ou* pal. Cigarettes? Cocoa?"

"Why don't you pay your bail and – – – – out of here?" The piggish eyes stared balefully down at him.

"Waste of money," cackled Solly. "Besides, I's *mos* here for a purpose, reckon and think." He winked slyly. "Reckon and think, we's going to make a bow, *mos*." He carried his boastfulness like an offering of good faith, forged credentials that would admit him into the society of great powers.

"Crack," said Butcherboy, and a hand as wide as a paddle-blade flicked out nonchalantly and swatted the little man away, sending him staggering among the legs of men around them. The column of prisoners, disrupted, eddied and undulated, and a guard came running up, shouting.

Solly extricated himself from the shuffling legs. Somebody aimed an unseen kick at him and he bounced up, piping, "Who the blerry hell did that? Just tell me, man. Just tell me."

The guard caught him by the collar and pushed him into line, shouting, "You can tell me if you want to get into trouble, you bogger. You can tell me," while Solly cried, "My boss, my *baas*."

The disrupted centre of the column sorted itself and straightened out again, and everybody became silent as the guards came up the length of the assembly, counting the men off in fours. When the count was over and the guards satisfied that nobody was missing, the column shuffled slowly forward towards the grille across the front of the yard.

All the stars had gone and the sky was flat white, starting to turn blue with the light from the sun which none of them would see until midday, when it would be overhead. The brightening morning slid gradually over the rough concrete and brownstone blocks of the walls and the high, barred gate of the yard started to throw narrow patterns of parallel shadows onto the ground before it.

Now two kitchen-squad convicts were bringing the morning porridge, carrying the many-tiered tray built into a framework like a sedan-chair, jogging and shuffling on their feet to ease the load on their hands, while they waited for the gate in the grille to be unlocked. Then they stamped forward and left the rack of tin bowls inside the gate, and the column of prisoners moved forward, each man taking a bowl.

Just then a clerk came into the square outside the yard and started to call out the names of those who had to appear in court that morning. At once a ripple of protest ran through the ranks of prisoners.

"Hey, we didn't have no breakfast yet, man," somebody cried.

"We got to eat first, *mos.*"

"They can't do this, hey."

The section-guard turned and bawled, "Shut up. Hold your – – – – jaws. You think this is a – – – – ing bioscope?" He turned to the clerk and said, "What's this, man? These people are getting their grub now."

The clerk shrugged. "I was told to get the court cases. The truck's waiting for them."

The guard said, shaking his head, "The way they run this place." He turned back to the waiting prisoners. "Awright. Those whose names are called, get your pap. The rest of you boggers wait."

The men whose names were called went through the gate and squatted against the wall of the square to eat. The rest of the column was shambling forward now, collecting the bowls of whitish porridge, and turning to haunch down along one side of the yard. Digging their fingers into the thick, pasty corn, they shovelled it into their mouths.

"Listen, pal, spare me a little of your sugar, please, man."

"Jussus. If you got money you can buy your own blerry sugar."

"Spent my last cent on tobacco, pal. I'll trade you a butt for some sugar."

"This crack. Those whites get sugar *and* milk. – – – – ing pig's food."

"Beans and pap. Beans and pap. That's all the – – – – govvermen' give you in this place."

"And a chunk of meat big as a thumb, twice a week with the lunch-time beans and rice."

"Well, somes johns is lucky they got some cash. Buy tin of corn beef, or sardines or pilchards."

"Pilchards. Listen, mate, here's nothing but pap and beans. So what does my old woman do? Send me – – – – pilchards every day. Every – – – – day pilchards. Take your pick, pal. Pap or pilchards. True as God, I'm sick as hell of pap, but I'm sicker of blerry pilchards."

"Hey, I say, slow with that sugar, hey. Got to las' till next or'er day."

"I'm going to order me a tin of can fruit next time."

"Jam las' longer, man."

"Once you open it you can't eat the whole tin, can you? You got to keep it, and then the dirt get into the stuff. Can fruit you can finish straight, don't I say? Make your stomach work, too."

"*Ja*. Man get tight as hell eating blerry pap and beans every day."

"You baskets is satisfied with nothing. What you expeck? A – – – – menu so you can pick and choose? Pap is pap. Is okay by me."

"Is okay by you. You not use to nothing better, don't I say? You blerry farm boys."

"Say, *ou*, spare me a little of the condense' milk, man."

"– – – – off. You reckon I'm a millerneer?"

George Adams, sitting with his back against the wall, surrounded by fellow prisoners, ate only a few mouthsful of the corn mush and then found himself unable to take any more. He thought, the trouble is you've got to eat this stuff or go hungry; unless the people outside send in something better. The committee might see to that, he told himself. Besides, he wanted to have a shower, and he had an idea he had better take it then, before breakfast was over, not knowing what was going to happen afterwards.

He was about to put his bowl aside, feeling a little ashamed of offering the leftovers to anybody else, when a hand like a peeled branch fastened onto his arm and he looked aside into the grinning, puckered face under a scarred peppercorn head.

"Pally," Solly cried, "You not *mos* going to throw that stuff away, is you?"

"I don't want it," George Adams said.

"You just give it to me, mate. Waste not, want not, like they say."

"That's okay, pal."

"T'anks, *dankie*, my mate."

Somebody called, "Hey, Solly, you bummed three blerry plates awready."

"What, you jealous?" the little man cackled between gulps at the mush.

"*Ghod.* So – – – – ing small, where the hell you put it, Solly?"

And the little man slapped his belly under the floppy shirt, with a greasy hand, and cackled again. He said to George Adams, "These burgs. A lot of blerry baskets. Now I and you, we got brains and understanding, hey?" He tapped his corrugated forehead with a finger as horrible as a witch's. "Me and you got brains, reckon and think, *ou* pal." He winked, grinning toothlessly. "They reckon *ou* Solly's a small-timer. But we know diff'rent, don't I say?"

"Sure, sure, pal," George Adams said smiling.

"He's *bedonerd*, crazy," a man said.

"Listen, you baskets," Solly piped at them. "What you all know?" He swallowed some mush. "*Ou* Solly know more about things and can do more than you boggers. Just you reckon and think." And he added quietly. "And these white men will see, too."

"What you going to do, Solly?" somebody jeered. "Break out?"

Solly made a gobbling sound of laughter in his throat. "Break out? Who want to break out, me with only a twenty-

57

day or something like that to do if they find me guilty? And three meals a day and free board and lodging on top of it? Break out? *Garn.*" He cackled again, and turned back to his eating.

George Adams patted the little man's shoulder and then rose, picking his way through the squatting prisoners and the spilled mush and the smell of bodies, walking under the warming, electric-yellow sunlight in the yard, towards the shower-room.

The shower-room, open to the yard, was under the balcony to the upper floor, and there was a row of chipped washbowls along one side and the showers on the other.

A nude boy with curly hair and the sharp face of a mouse, with the line drawing of "The Saint" tattooed on his right arm, was drying himself with a scrap of rag. He looked up and winked at George Adams.

"You awright, papa?"

"Yes, man," George Adams said, unbuttoning his trousers. He was in a hurry, in case the prisoners were called to assemble again.

The boy smiled back and saluted, going out stark naked, trailing his clothes in one hand.

George Adams stepped under the rush of water and shuddered for a moment as the iciness attacked his skin, and then when his body adjusted to the chill, started to rub himself all over.

He would have to organise some razor-blades, he thought. He did not like growing a beard. He was under the shower for hardly a minute, when he heard the guard shouting, "All you new people who came in last night, come on out."

Oh, Lord, now what? he thought. He could hear the guard's impatient snapping, and he dried himself as best he could with his towel, and then pulled on his trousers. The other newcomers were already filing out through the gate into the square, and George Adams, jerking on his shoes, irritably cursed the guard, cursed the jail, cursed the whole country that was like a big stone prison, anyway.

He was the last one out into the square, and the guard, standing at the gate to count them off, looked at him with eyes that were cold and dark and bitter as midnight in winter, and said, "What the hell, you sleeping on your – – – – feet?" George Adams went past the guard, not looking at him and cursed him again in his mind.

9

Now they were lined up against a wall in the square, watched by a dark guard in a washed-out topi, feeling the sun in their faces, like the warm touch of a woman's hand. But George Adams thought, It's like waiting for the firing squad. He asked, without looking at the one beside him, "What's all this, mate?"

"Doctor. As if a doctor going to be any good."

The words shot from the speaker's mouth like pips being spat out, and turning his head, George Adams recognised the boy, Albert March, The Casbah Kid, who was there pending his trial for murder. The small, smooth, gnawed face with its wispy moustache, like that of a slum child who had decorated his upper lip to appear grown-up, stared ahead out of wet, hooded, pebbly eyes. George Adams saw that his mouth was swollen, the lip split and raw.

"How you, pal?" George Adams asked, trying to speak in the low, lipless voice which seemed to come naturally to prisoners, when in the presence of authority.

"Okay." The word was hardly a reply to a question, more a reluctant acknowledgement that a query had been made, and George Adams sensed the invisible armour drawn around the boy who seemed as unapproachable as a wave-washed rock.

"What happened to your mouth?"

"Nothing."

"You going to have the doctor look at it?"

"Is okay."

George Adams had tried to force conversation from the boy, but it was like tackling a safe with a soft tool: the combination was scattered and the door clamped shut, turning the poor edge of the jemmy.

He was about to try again, when the guard in the topi said sharply, "Hup! Any of you men sick?"

The doctor was coming through the archway from the adjacent yard. He wore civilian clothes and had grey hair, like damp sand, and carried a stethoscope in one hand like a whip. None of the prisoners moved.

The guard saluted and said, "Morning, doctor. Everybody all right."

The doctor nodded, and his eyes, pouched and watery, as if they were being preserved in little cups of formaldehyde, swivelled and ran along the line of men. Then he nodded again to the guard, and went on past them towards another section of the prison.

"Well, that *mos* take care of us," one of the men in the line mocked, and the guard growled at them. The man said insolently, "Okay, *mos*, man, Corpy," which was the name they gave Coloured warders. "We all brown people, hey."

The guard glared back at him and for a moment his lips writhed like squirming caterpillars. Then his face went stolid and he snapped, "Shut up. Back to the yard."

Inside the yard a squad of prisoners was washing down the concrete floor, running from the tap in the rear with buckets of water and dashing them about merrily, while others scrubbed energetically with hard brooms, the whole operation becoming a game. Others were cleaning out the tin bowls and stacking them at the gate for collection by the kitchen squad; the leftovers of mush had been dumped into large drums for removal to the pig farms.

Around the drums, the prison cat, sleek and glistening with health, was sniffing and purring, its shining tail raised like a flag-pole, its tongue whisking pinkly at the congealed dribbles of paste.

Other prisoners were sweeping out the cells under the

eyes of cell bosses, emptying night-soil buckets into the open drains in the square, while the section-guard stood near the grille, scratching the back of his hand, until, looking up he found George Adams before him.

"*Ja?* What is your trouble?" The voice had the expressionless sound of a dripping faucet. This guard was heavy and paunchy and seemed to be constructed from a series of soft, smoothly joined sacs, and he had a plump, smooth, healthy pink face, like a Santa Claus with a blonde moustache instead of a snow-white beard; in the outwardly jolly face the eyes were pale and washed-out and silvery, much like imitation pearls, and cold as quicksilver.

"I didn't get any blankets and a mat when I came in yesterday," George Adams told him, looking at the bleached eyes.

"So?"

"Can I have them now, sir?"

The hard eyes assumed a scratchy quality and seemed to rasp over George Adams. "Sir? You should know that there is no – *sir* in this place. Here you say *Boss*, hear me?"

George Adams continued to look at the plump red face. The guard had his thick, pink thumbs tucked into his belt, and his plump fingers tapped gently on the polished leather. Something like an impaled worm writhed under the pudgy skin in the guard's throat, but the eyes did not change. "Did you hear me?"

George Adams said, "I heard you, sir." He was thinking, Is this nose going to get snotty over such a small matter?

But the bitter eyes held him for a further moment, and then moved away, and the guard bawled for the store boy who shuffled forward, looking nervous and obsequious. The guard said: "Get two blankets and a mat and give it to this *jong*, and don't be so blerry particular either." To George Adams he said, "*Jong*, here you better not keep yourself *slim*, clever. There's trouble waiting for you if you keep yourself too clever." Then, as an afterthought: "Let's see your card."

George Adams drew the blue card from his hip pocket. Near him he was aware of silence. The silence spread like spilt treacle as the little drama unfolded, and the men who had been carrying water put down their buckets, and others leaned on their brooms, everybody waiting and watching. You didn't talk back to a guard, and George Adams had done so, even in a small way, and they all waited for the storm of authority which seemed to be building up.

The guard took the card and looked at it with the faded, silvery eyes. Then he said, his voice heavy and dry, "Illegal organisation, *ja*? You're one of *those*, hey? Bloody Communis', stocking up trouble everywhere. Awright, I got an eye on you, mister. Just *pas op*, watch out." The plump face was immobile as a papier mâché mask, and only the lips under the blonde moustache moved as he spoke. He handed the card back.

The store boy returned and dumped a mat and two folded blankets on the damp ground at George Adams's feet. George Adams looked at him and said coldly: "You see any necessity to lay the stuff in the wet?"

The man giggled nervously and then looked away, and beside George Adams the guard's voice exploded: "Hey, you bloody robbish. Pick up that stuff and – – – – off before there's trouble."

George Adams felt cold in spite of the sun on his back and neck, something smouldered inside and his heart was beating against his ribs. He did not look at the guard's face, but bent down and gathered up the gear. He did not look at the guard or say anything, but carried the rolled mat and blankets towards his cell, passing other men in the yard, passing the brutal faces and the depraved faces, the young faces and the lined faces, the hopeless faces and the stubborn faces, and suddenly he felt better again and winked as he passed, and the silent men looked curiously at him, and a few grinned and winked back, too.

Behind him, the guard looked over at Butcherboy, the brute man, who lounged against the rough, stone-constructed wall of one side of the yard, and smiled a wintery smile, saying, "He's *mos* one of those *slim* men. He's looking for trouble."

And Butcherboy shifted his great shoulders against the wall and grinned, saying, "Old boss, he *is* looking for trouble. A clever."

10

When George Adams emerged from the cell again, the rest of the prisoners were seating themselves in rows on the ground opposite, in the shadow of the wall. Officially, this was the exercise period, but on some pretext or other, the men were forced to sit through the whole period until lunchtime. Some of the hard cases, assuming a dubious superiority, did not join the rows, but lounged in the doorways of their cells, smoking and conversing quietly.

At the same time, a clerk had appeared in the square again, and once more names were being called from a paper which he held in his hand. Men were leaving the rows to go out through the gate, and George Adams, buttoning his shirt which he had pulled on now, heard his own name and walked towards the gate after the others, and going out, he felt rather than saw the fat guard's pale eyes scouring him from above the hard-etched kink which was a grin on his lips.

George Adams thought, with a prick of triumph, These boggers don't like a man talking back at them; I bet that Fatty is more worried about me than he is about anybody else in the yard.

In the square the warder marched them off past the Headquarters Block and past the White Remand Section where the prisoners, most of them in shorts and bathing trunks, sunned themselves or chatted with their guard. There were very few of them, compared with the numbers in the other section.

Then through an archway into another square between the White Hard-labour Section and the row which consisted of the dispensary, the sick-bay, the stores and the kitchen for the staff. In a corner of the square, a gang of white convicts in khaki, wearing goggles and heavy gloves, sat on the ground behind a wire screen and pounded into chips small rocks brought from the quarries.

The double file of prisoners reached the outer wall of the jail at the other end of the square. There was a high steel grille, topped with three strands of barbed wire, separating them from the door in the wall. The door was also screened off by a partition, so that only the guard at the gate and the two convicts who assisted him could see who came in.

The escort collected their ID cards and handed them through the grille to the guard who also wore a holstered pistol. After a wait the guard started calling names, and the prisoners went forward to collect whatever had been brought for them.

George Adams was given a tin of beef, a tin of cocoa, fifty cigarettes and a cake of perfumed soap and a tube of toothpaste, all in a brown paper bag which he accepted happily, wondering whether they had come from his landlady or the committee.

He guessed he would find out on visiting day, but he realised that he had owed his landlady two weeks rent when he had been arrested, and that she was probably too broke or too browned off to spend money on this stuff.

Behind the grille the convicts were cutting loaves of bread lengthways, one cut down the middle, to look for contraband, then passing them in.

When the transfer was completed, they followed the escort again, with laden arms or stuffed pockets, back to their section. On the way, George Adams put the flat box of cigarettes into his shirt pocket and rolled the rest of the goodies tight in the bag.

Then, on his way towards his cell once more, he felt a thick hand laid casually on his shoulder and halted, feeling hot, sour breath against his neck, while a thick voice, distorted by a damaged throat, said, "Howsit, pally? You got something nice there for us?"

George Adams looked aside and up and into the blood-flecked, gorilla eyes and the heavy, red, rubbery lips peeled back to reveal broken, stained and mossy teeth like desecrated tombstones, grinning out of the bludgeoned and badly-repaired, stubbly face.

"You got something nice there for us, pal?"

The harsh, carious breath fanned him, and George Adams was reminded of overturned dustbins in the grime-slippery lobbies of mouldering tenements and the smell of latrine buckets in hot cells. He said carefully, "Just some stuff my people sent me."

"That's real wake-up," Butcherboy said huskily, and George Adams felt the big hand close like an iron grab on his shoulder. He stood very still and waited for the next move.

"Well, *ou* pal, let us see what you got for us in that bag, *ou* pal."

Around them the muttered conversation of the squatting prisoners evaporated slowly and the atmosphere became taut as a harp-string as all eyes turned on them. In the stretched silence somebody giggled nervously, and the sound took on an exaggerated character, like the smashing of crockery, and George Adams, exploding into anger, glared into the bloodshot eyes as he shouted, "– – – – off!"

Something like a sigh now swept through the onlookers, and everybody seemed to tense with the anticipation of violence. At the grille at the end of the yard, the guard did not move from his place, and George Adams, knowing that he was there, watching, realised now that this was the guard's way of repaying what he considered insolence, and that it was of no use appealing to him.

George Adams could feel his mouth quivering with rage, and his shoulder had gone numb, clamped in the steel-wire fingers. He heard the throaty voice ask mockingly curious: "What was that what you said, pal?"

"– – – – off," George Adams said, raising his voice again, so that everybody could hear, thinking at the same time, This bastard can break your neck like a match, why don't you just play it small?

"So. *Ach so*," the throaty voice laughed, and the hard, blunt head turned towards the group of henchmen who lounged, grinning, in a doorway, with even the face of The Casbah Kid twisted into a reluctant grimace as he slouched on the fringes.

"This little man, he like to talk back," Butcherboy told them, laughing hoarsely. "He's *mos* a clever. Like to talk back to big johnnies."

The horrid face turned back to George Adams. "Such a short-arse, too." The ape-like eyes moved in their deep sockets, and discovered the bulge of the cigarette-box in the shirt pocket.

"Let's see now, man. Tobacco, hey? Maybe, if they's what I smoke, I won't break your – – – – ing neck." And the free hand came up towards the pocket and George Adams saw the tattooed arm, ropy with muscle, and fingers thick as cables with their half moons of dirt under the nails. "You's a shot, *mos*. Cigarettes and all."

George Adams thought, I'm going to kick him in the balls, and hope for the best; I'll probably land up in hospital. He moved his legs slightly, without betraying any sign of his intention. He was still holding his parcel and prepared himself to drop it as soon as he kneed the big man.

And then somebody else said jovially, "What do you need, Butcherboy? Picking on respectable people, like."

Both Butcherboy and George Adams recognised the voice, and looked aside to where the tall, lean, knife-blade form of Yusef the Turk had moved up. The sleek handsome head was cocked and the face smiled, showing the even dentures, white as new enamel in the swarthy face.

"Turk," Butcherboy said, without relaxing his hold on George Adams. "Turk, this is not your business, *mos*. *Ou* Turk, man, you's in the wrong place, man."

"Why, Butcher?" Yusef the Turk asked easily. "Wrong place? Hell, man, we's all here together in the wrong place, don't I say?"

"You know what I mean, man. Me and this *juba*, we's *mos* got business."

"Business," Yusef the Turk laughed. "This is *good* people, man. Not your kind, not my kind, even. You know this john? No." The easy voice changed suddenly, and the Turk said dangerously, "Leave him."

Butcherboy did not move, but the reddish eyes contracted into their folds of grimy flesh, and peered out between the narrowed lids like predatory creatures in ambush. "Turk, I'm just giving you a fair warning, hey." The husky voice was menacing.

In the yard the watching prisoners stirred again, and Butcherboy's henchmen, Brakes Peterson, Squinteye Samuels, Pinks, Moos and others, straightened and edged instinctively into line of battle. The Casbah Kid flicked out his tongue and licked his battered lip, his eyes on Butcherboy, and a hand closed over the skewer in his pocket.

But Yusef the Turk ignored them and said, "Butcher, you been bossing this yard a long time, don't I say?"

"*Ja*, and so?"

"You *mos* catch wire with the small boys, don't I say?"

"*Ja*, and so?"

"So I'm telling you this is a pally of mine. Leave him."

Butcherboy released a gust of bad breath and shook his head slowly. "Turk," he said. "Turk, I's sorry for you. Turk, you getting too big for this yard, so I'm going to do something about it, hey."

"Any time you say, Butcherboy."

"Maybe you might *mos* move over to my cell one night."

Yusef the Turk smiled a dangerous smile. "Why not, then?"

"Is okay, then."

George Adams now said to the lean man, "Forget it, Yusef, man."

"Is okay, pal," Yusef the Turk said. "And maybe *ou* Butcherboy will let go your shoulder now, hey?"

The tiny eyes stared at Yusef the Turk who smiled back, and just then the triangle outside the square clanged and clanged, and the guard was shouting, "Fall in, fall in," so that the general movement of the prisoners, rising to assemble, broke the tension like the snap of a fishing-line.

Butcherboy relaxed his grip on George Adams's shoulder and removed his hand. He said, "We will talk about it some more, Turk," and Yusef the Turk chuckled.

11

Now they were all assembled for inspection, the short ones in front and the tall men behind, everybody in files of four, holding the blue ID cards so that the Superintendent of the jail could read their names in case he had anything to say to anybody. The guard walked along the front rank, his eyes chill as new frost, and as pale, slapping the side of his leg with the strap of his truncheon.

He asked suspiciously, "Any complaints?" But nobody spoke up or moved out, and he went down the line again towards the gate, saying, "Caps off, caps off."

The Superintendent arrived and the section-guard unlocked the gate for him, stamped elaborately to attention, saluting stiffly, and said, "Two hundred and sixty-nine awaiting trial. Everything all right, Major."

The Super returned the salute with a gesture of his swagger-stick and started down the line with the guard trailing behind.

The Super was a very tall, thin, bony man with big knobbly joints looking as if he had been roughly carved out of knotty wood. The prisoners had secretly nicknamed him "Major Planks," and he had a dry, brittle face like crumpled pink tissue-paper with holes torn in it for eyes, and a horizontal crease left for a mouth.

He went along the column of men, peered into the shower-room, and then made a sound like a grunt. Apparently satisfied with everything, he turned about and headed back for the gate which the guard held open for him.

As soon as he had disappeared, a mutter of talk broke out and the prisoners relaxed.

"Old basket had – – – – all to say this morning. Must be in a good mood."

"Hell, is because he don't have to serve meat with the lunch today. He's *mos* always in a bad mood when they got to give away the govvermen's meat."

"Well, *ou* Fatso did get the blerry count right today, anyway, don't I say?"

"*Ja.* Never knew the basket could count proper. Ha. Ha."

George Adams was rubbing his shoulder where Butcherboy had gripped him. It felt numb and a little painful, and he thought, That big ox, I wish I'd given him the bloody knee. He kept his eyes on the cell door, in case somebody sneaked in to filch. He thought he would divide the tin of beef among all of them who occupied the cell. They could all have some cocoa too, but it would have to be cold; he had heard that they only issued hot water with the breakfast.

The fat guard was shouting the inevitable, "Fall in, fall in," and everybody was moving towards the gate to collect the lunch, the toughs pushing their way to the front to get the beans and rice while the food was still warm. You had hardly eaten the breakfast, when they served the lunch. By three-thirty in the afternoon they served the supper and everybody was locked up.

When George Adams eventually received his bowl, he sought out Yusef the Turk and sat down beside him.

The lean man was shovelling rice and beans into his mouth and chewing without enthusiasm. He winked at George Adams and said, between swallows, "How you, Professor?"

"Okay," George Adams said, tasting the poorly cooked food. "This stuff."

"*Ja.* That basket hurt you?"

"Squeezed my shoulder a little." George Adams masticated some beans and added, "What you interfere for, hey?"

Yusef the Turk grinned at him. "Isn't you glad, mate? That giant could have torn off your arm, man."

"I'm glad awright, I reckon. But now he's going to lay in *your* tracks." George Adams glanced across to where Butcherboy was eating, surrounded by his associates. "I don't reckon you can pull him up much, Yussy."

"Yussy can look after himself, Professor. Just *you* keep out of his way. You not his weight, hey."

"Not his weight? I don't reckon you's heavy enough."

Yusef the Turk spat out a bean. "This – – – – stuff is hard as stones."

George Adams asked, "Well, what for did you interfere? You said *mos* every man for himself in this place."

"*Ja.* Maybe is for *jubas* like me and Butcherboy and the res' of these *skolly*-boy hoodlums." He laughed. "People like you, we got to look after, *mos.*"

"Thanks. *Dankie.*" George Adams said. "But Butcherboy will murder you, man. He talked big to you, and I reckon you also talked big, so he got to make good his word, don't I say?"

Yusef the Turk said, "Don't worry, Professor. He won't *murder* me, no, pally." He chewed and swallowed. "Maybe I will land in the sick-bay or hospital, but a man sleep on a bed there, and get better treatment than here."

A flock of pigeons dropped out of the sky and landed on the parapet of the cell-block.

George Adams put his bowl aside; he could not take any more of the prison food. Besides, he had remembered the can of bully. He said, "That's a nice way to get better treatment."

Yusef the Turk said easily, "Listen here, pal. There johns serving time working on the quarries, and they can't stand it any more after a time. So they cut the strings in their heels to get away from that place. Or maybe they tackle a guard and get solitary or brought here for extra charges. Just to get a little easier treatment, hey."

"I heard about that," George Adams said.

"Well, don't worry about your pal Yussy, man. If that Butcherboy want to take it up, okay. If he don't, well then, okay." He wiped his fingers on the edge of his bowl. "I wonder why my goose didn't bring me no stuff today. Eating this crack. She know she got to bring me a diet every day. I'll kick her blerry backside, I get out of here."

He put the bowl aside, then removed his dentures and started to clean them with a match.

The pigeons, blue-grey in the sunlight, sailed from the roof and dropped to the floor of the yard, strutted with smooth-feathered importance among the fallen scraps of food, their sharp beaks pecking skilfully past their pouting breasts.

A man, a newcomer who had arrived the previous day, now set his bowl aside, leaned forward and made soft, crooning bird sounds, extending a ragged arm towards the pigeons. He was dressed in tattered jacket, patched trousers and disintegrating shoes, and he had a flabby body and a flabby, liquor-bloated, sagging face, like a half-filled penny balloon. The unshaven, pouchy mouth smiled and his soft, gentle calling came strangely from it.

"Cooo-rrr. Cooo-rrr," the man called quietly to the birds.

Then, as everybody watched, the pigeons rose on fluttering wings to settle on the ragged arm and shoulders, so that the man, rising to his feet, looked like some strange mythological being, half-feathers-half-human.

The man crooned to the birds and reached out with a cracked, blunt finger to stroke the pearl-grey, blue-green backs with the touch as gentle as light. The pigeons pushed and shuffled over the arm and shoulders of the man and he stood there, whispering to them, like some soiled and ragged Saint Francis.

"Do you know, boys," he said to those who watched him, "that there are over six hundred different kinds of these birds?" He smiled, stroking the smooth, silky backs. "I know pigeons, hey. Use to have a flock of my own, I did." The pigeons moved and pushed all over his upper body, so that his head emerged from a ruff of birds.

"Pigeons," he went on. "Pigeons, they say, keep the same mate for life, friends. Hell, they's almost like humans. Listen to me, pals. A pigeon – female, that is – lay two white eggs and she feed the little ones on what is called pigeon's milk. It come out of her crop, like."

He chuckled. "*Ja*, use to have lot of pigeons, I did. Fantails, Pouters, all kinds, hey. Use to go in for racing. Hey, those birds could fly." He stood there, chatting, while around him the prisoners looked on in a mixture of awe and curiosity.

"Good homing pigeon weigh about sixteen ounces," the ragged man explained with authority. "You know they can go up to ninety-seven miles a hour? And that, weather permitting, they can travel from five hundred to seven hundred miles in a day? That's between daybreak and nightfall, min' you. *Ja*, pals, you ask me. I know *mos* about pigeons, man."

He stopped talking and crooned to the birds again, and they crooned back at him, and then he raised the feather-laden arm and seemed to say something to them, and the birds rose from him with a rustle of wings, heading towards the flat blue sky.

When the bowls had been washed and stacked for removal to the kitchens, everybody was returned to the cells and locked up until the evening meal. In one of the cells prisoners began to sing *White Christmas*.

George Adams said, grinning, "Everybody's dreaming of a white Chris'mas."

They had unrolled their mats and spread the blankets, and the three men who shared the cell with them had produced their battered pack of cards and had started to play.

Yusef the Turk said, scratching his ribs under his shirt: "Chris'mas, Chris'mas. One day's like another in this place. 'Cept they give you extra bit of meat on Chris'mas day and the Salvation Army ban' come to play." He found something under his shirt and looked at it. "They got to spray this place. – – – – creepers." He cracked the louse between his thumb-nails. He laughed. "Got to spray this place for Chris'mas."

George Adams took out his new box of cigarettes and tore off the ceilophane covering, broke the seal and offered the box to Yusef the Turk. The lean man took one and snapped his lighter. George Adams held out the cigarettes to the card-players.

"Smoke up, pallies," he said. "There's lots."

One of the men took a cigarette and George Adams said, "Take another, man." The man grinned and took a second cigarette. "What you in for?" George Adams asked the old question.

"They caught us in a grocery shop," the man said. He had a round brown face, and he smiled so that the face opened up from ear to ear, showing red gums, like a sliced watermelon. "We was all together."

"Three blerry musketeers," Yusef the Turk said, grinning. "Grocery shop."

The other men took two cigarettes each, and one of them stuck one in his mouth and the other behind his ear, shuffling the pack and tilting his head while his cigarette was lighted for him.

It was hot in the cell again, and the air thickened, hanging like a solid veil, undulating with tobacco smoke. George Adams removed his shirt and fanned his face with it.

He said, "Wish the wind would come up a little." Then he added: "I got a tin of bully. You reckon we ought to open it?"

"No," Yusef the Turk said. "Supper is about a quarter loaf of bread and a mug of cawfee. We can eat the bully with that, it'll go down nice."

Along the row they were now singing *Silver Bells*. From the gateway of the yard the guard bawled for silence, and the song staggered to a close.

"Just bread?" George Adams asked.

"With a dab of jam, like," Yusef the Turk told him. "Use to be fat, but the Moslems and Indians had to get ghee. I reckon is was *mos* too much trouble for them to separate the ghees from the fats every day, so now every bogger get jam. Also, is was a small loaf, 'bout a quarter-pound each, what we used to call cat's-head. Now they just cut up a pound loaf, see? Blerry cat-head with a spoonful of jam."

"Prisoners ought to objeck," George Adams said. "Strike for better diet, *mos*."

"*Ja*," Yusef the Turk grinned. "You tell them, Professor."

"That Butcherboy didn't make any move again," George Adams said. "You reckon he'll forget it?"

"Not him," said the other, shaking his head. He yawned and went on: "He got to meet me. His hangers-on expeck it, see? If he don't come up, he lose his place in this yard."

"He's such a big basket," George Adams said.

Yusef the Turk laughed. "The bigger they come, the harder they fall."

He thought, feeling sleepy with the heat writhing around them, What a waste; here they got us fighting each other like dogs. George Adams did not have any regrets about his arrest. You did what you decided was the right thing, and then accepted the consequences. He had gone to meetings and had listened to the speeches, had read a little, and had come to the conclusion that what had been said was right. He thought, falling into dreamless sleep, There's a limit to being kicked in the backside . . . .

12

The grinding of the key in the lock woke him, and he sat up, blinking with eyes suddenly exposed to light. The others were rising, taking down their tin mugs from the hook on the window-screen. George Adams rose to his feet too, and rubbed sleep from his eyes. The door thumped open and the guard was on his way to unlock the next one.

"Have a nice nap, mate?" asked Yusef the Turk.

"I dropped off," George Adams said. "Listen, I haven't got a mug."

"Hell, mate, you better not ask for one now. Old Fats is going to go *bedonerd*, crazy."

"Why?" George Adams asked him. "They should have given me the bloody thing when I came in, don't I say? Is not *my* fault."

The other three had gone out, and George Adams and Yusef the Turk followed them. "I'm not going to let these baskets get away with anything," George Adams said.

"Okay, Professor. But watch *ou* Fatso, hey."

The prisoners were forming up in twos for the coffee and bread which waited for them at the gate, served by two convicts from the kitchen.

George Adams broke rank and walked up to the fat guard who was watching the issue of the supper. He looked up as George Adams approached, and his eyes did not change, but maintained their gravelly look.

"What is your trouble now?" asked the frozen voice.

"I didn't get a mug when I came in."

"So it's you again, hey?" The blonde moustache twitched slightly. "That's just too bad, *jong*. No mug, no coffee."

"I'm entitled to a mug, isn't it?" George Adams asked, looking at the yellow-lashed eyes. "I can't help it if the man on duty didn't hand out the stuff."

The eyes seemed to grow dark with anger, and the ruddiness of the smooth plump face flushed deeper. "You *donder*," the guard shouted. "Who the hell you talking to? You think I let any *skolly* talk to me like he was a white man? – – – – off, out of my sight."

George Adams did not move, but continued to look into the flushed face. He was thinking, Be damned if I'm going to let him get away with it. They expect you to crawl for everything: Please, boss, can I have this? Please, boss, can I have that? He said, "Well, why don't they run this jail proper?"

The guard's face writhed like a puddle of boiling lava. He was losing his temper, firstly because this piece of crap had the audacity to exchange words with him – that was bad, because if you found yourself having to explain things, they got the idea you were losing your grip; secondly, here was this man criticising the administration – that was the beginning of rebellion and mutiny. Finally, this was one of those agitators who went around stirring up things against authority.

"So you one of those *slim* men, hey? A clever darky." The tone was quieter now, dropping to its original iciness as the fat guard regained his composure. But it was all the more dangerous, for this man's authority was enforced with the shock of ice, rather than with the sear of white heat. He froze resistance, rather than melted it, and that method allowed him to maintain a sort of frigid superiority.

He was aware that the distribution of the bitter black coffee and the hunks of bread had come to a standstill, and that everybody was watching to see what would happen.

Then the store boy shuffled forward, saying, "There's a spare mug here, *baas*." He gestured with the mug, not looking at the guard, and the guard said, "Who the hell called you to do anything?" But he did not object when George Adams took the mug; neither when George Adams gave the man two cigarettes in exchange. But he sensed the defiance, and turned angrily on the waiting column of prisoners.

"What the hell you standing there, gaping? Take your blerry food and get back to your cells." He realised that he had been defeated, and it rankled him.

The column began to move forward and George Adams walked towards the back of the line. Some of the men stared at him, and he caught the porcine glare of Butcherboy who stood lounging in a cell door, waiting for his supper to be brought to him. His mind, rusty, but treacherous as a forgotten bear-trap, wondered whether he could do the *baas* a favour by dealing with this clever.

Near the middle of the column, Yusef the Turk called out softly to George Adams, "Duck in here, pal." Men made a place for him, grinning widely, while Solly, who stood by Yusef the Turk, cackled quietly, "Pally, you took *ou* Fatty down, *mos*, man."

And even Brakes Peterson with his half-face, the other half like a roasted side of beef, said in a lipless whisper, "One day somebody going to do something bad to that fat-arsed basket."

Butcherboy, overhearing this, sensed a threatened shift of allegiance, and he told himself that matters would have to be handled quickly. But he would have to fix that Yusef the Turk first. With The Turk out of the way, the other would be helpless. *Ja*, he would have to see to that Turk.

A little way further back, The Casbah Kid took hold of the sharpened skewer in the pocket of his jeans, thumb and two fingers curled about the ring end in a grip like a vice, and his mouth bent one degree out of line, in the phantom of a smile.

13

The morning was bright in the yard, and the iron grille which formed the end wall threw its pattern of parallel grey lines and garish rectangles onto the concrete floor. Overhead the sky was a hard enamel blue smudged with a coppery smear of sun. There was no sign of a breeze, and beyond the stern hard stone and PWD paint of the prison, the outline of the flat mountain was clear and sharp as a cleaver against the sky.

The section-guard was in the square outside the yard, but near the grille, talking to another guard who was stationed there. The three convicts from the Isolation Block opposite the Remand Section, were exercising in the square, walking round and round in a circle.

The tap at the upper end of the yard had been opened and water ran along the shallow trench down the middle of the concrete floor where the prisoners were busy washing their clothes. The slapping sounds of wet material beaten on the stone, flop-flop-flopped through the murmur of voices and occasional laughter. Some of the men were stark naked, having decided to wash every scrap of rag they possessed, others squatted in shorts or trousers, everybody scrubbing and pummelling in two lines, facing each other across the running trench. Those who were not washing lounged about and smoked or talked.

Yusef the Turk wrung out the shirt he had washed and rose stiffly from his place at the gutter, and carried it over to the wash-line of wire which had been strung between the banister of the gallery steps and the grille. Having draped the shirt over the line, he sat down with his back to the wall, and proceeded to watch it.

He watched it unwaveringly and intently, for he knew that to move his gaze for only a few seconds might mean its complete and utter disappearance. Others who had also hung up washing were sitting around, staring at their clothes with trance-like devotion, waiting for the summer sun to do its work.

Sitting there, his eyes on the drying shirt, Yusef the Turk decided truculently that his mistress was a mean and inconsiderate bitch for not having brought him any clean laundry that week. There had not been a visit from her either, and there was a suspicion forming in his mind that she had thrown him over, now that he was safely in prison, and had taken up with someone else. He was wondering whether he should forget about her altogether, or go and see her to give her something to remember him by when he got out. It did not occur to him that he might be in jail for a very long time. While he was sitting there, thinking, he became aware of the anthropoid bulk of Butcherboy, who had slunk up beside him.

"Turk," Butcherboy said, and his voice was a growl deep down in the cavernous chest. "Turk."

"*Ja*," replied Yusef the Turk, without taking his eyes from the shirt suspended from the line. "You got something on your min'?"

He did not see the ragged-toothed grin on the flat, bristly face; only heard the rumbling voice. "This – – – – soap that they give out here is like stone. Turk, I hear *mos* you got a piece of real washing soap. I reckon to myself maybe you going to let me use it, Turk."

Yusef the Turk laughed, amused at the line of approach. He said, staring at the shirt, "Butcherboy, *ou* pal, I only just want to tell you two things, like. Number one is, you never did have no use for soap all your life. And number two is, I wouldn't lend you a fart in a crackhouse."

"Turk," Butcherboy said, still grinning balefully, "Turk, this yard is *mos* getting too small for us two together. You one of them big-shot burgs, hey. And I reckon to myself, is *mos* time you got to show what kin' of a big-shot you is. Don't I say?"

"Any time you say, Butcherboy."

"Okay, *ou* Turk. Tonight I reckon one of those baskets from my cell will move over to yours. Then you can move into mine, likely. Then we can settle this business. Okay?"

Yusef the Turk smiled at his shirt. He said, "Okay, pally."

"Tonight then, hey?"

"Tonight," said Yusef the Turk.

Butcherboy turned and made his way to where his henchmen and other attachments to his power were assembled in the shade, slapping aside obstructing bodies as he went. Yusef the Turk did not watch him go, but concentrated on his shirt which was now drying rapidly.

The heat danced in the yard, shimmering like sheets of badly-formed glass, and the prisoners who had nothing to do gathered in the shadow of the long wall, waiting for the inspection fall-in.

The prison cat undulated across the concrete, its tortoise-shell pelt gleaming in the sunlight, its tail waving like an antenna. It reached the trench where the water ran, drank briefly, and then went on through the bars of the grille.

George Adams came up to where Yusef the Turk sat, carrying his undervest over an arm, feeling the sun hot on his back through the single layer of his shirt.

He asked seriously, "What that john want now, Yussy?"

Yusef the Turk climbed to his feet and felt his shirt, then took it down from the line. George Adams was opening his cigarette-box, and he offered one to the other man.

"Just paying a visit, likely," Yusef the Turk said, smiling. "We going to settle this business tonight, in his cell."

"Tonight?" George Adams struck a match and they lighted up. "I'm going over with you."

"No need, pally. You keep out of it, hey."

"*You* reckon," George Adams told him. He felt a little worried. "You stuck your nose in when he was – – – – ing around with me, isn't it? If you had not, you would not be in this, *mos*." He blew a cone of smoke into the yellow sunlight. "So I want to go along, man."

Yusef the Turk said, "So I didn't *mos* like to see a john like you being pulled up by that basket. We got to look after you, Professor." He grinned, showing the dentures like cheap white porcelain.

George Adams said, "You and your every man for himself."

"*Ja*. Well, it look like *ou* Major Planks is on his way. There's the bell." The triangle in the square was clanging the fall-in.

14

The heat in the cell was solid. As Yusef the Turk would have said, you could reach out in front of your face, grab a handful of heat, fling it at the wall and it would stick. With over forty prisoners locked up in the middle of summer, the smell of sweat was heavy and cloying as the smell of death. The heat seemed packed in between the bodies of the men, like layers of cotton wool; like a thick sauce which moistened a human salad of accused petty thieves, gangsters, rapists, burglars, thugs, brawlers, dope peddlars, few of them strangers to the cells, many already depraved, and several old and abandoned, sucking hopelessly at the bitter, disintegrating butt-end of life.

Everybody was quiet that night, hardly noticing the heat. Words passed in whispers, instead of in an uproar which usually preceded the settling down for the night. Tension held the caserne in its taut grip.

Outside, the sun had dwindled away, leaving the lavender twilight to filter over the stone and iron of the prison. The guards had taken the last count of the day, and had handed over to the night shift. The warders now on duty noticed the silence only casually, the way one noticed a street light after dark, or the sheen on the ground after a rainfall, and it did not bother them.

Inside the caserne the bread and coffee had been hurriedly bolted or stored away for later consumption; the greasy decks of cards, the dice and the crude checker-games were not in evidence. Along the row of small cells, out of sight in the yard, and on the upper floor, silence mingled with the odour of bodies and the sticky heat.

George Adams did not like it. He felt nervous, and he did not like it at all. This was the country behind the coast-line of laws and regulations and labyrinthine legislation; a jungle of stone and iron, inhabited by jackals and hyenas, snarling wolves and trembling sheep, entrapped lions fighting off shambling monsters with stunted brains and bodies armoured with the hide of ignorance and brutality, trampling underfoot those who tried to claw their way from the clutch of the swamp.

And Butcherboy said, "Turk, I reckon we got to put you on trial."

Yusef the Turk stood loosely against the wall at one end of the caserne, with George Adams by him. He was smiling faintly with drooping lids, but despite the ease and the smile, his eyes were alert as sparks, and he was now sharp and tough and dangerous as a polished spear.

"Trial?" asked Yusef the Turk. "Hell, *ou* Butcher, I thought this was going to be a fair fight. Man to man."

A not uncommon occurrence in prison was the "trial", by the most depraved and brutalised inmates, of some unfortunate who might have raised their ire by rebellion, by boot-licking a guard, by squealing on fellow prisoners, or by provoking vengeance in some way or other. Mock courts, much more dangerous than real ones, were held in the cells and "sentence meted out".

There had been a "case" of a prisoner who had given offence to a cell boss and his gang. It had been said that he had complained to a guard, an unpardonable "crime". The gangsters "tried" him, found him guilty and sentenced him to – he was not told. That, as some sadistic refinement, they kept secret among themselves.

The terrified man died a thousand times over before, finally, unable to hold back weariness, he was forced to collapse in sleep. As he lay quaking through some unknown nightmare, a blanket was pressed over his head and face, and a half-dozen knives driven through the one in which he slept.

The next morning the guards found a dead man wrapped in a bloody blanket. No trace of blood on any of the rest of the packed humanity in the cell. There was no sign of a knife. Nobody had a knife, in spite of searches. The prison enquiry revealed nothing.

Butcherboy laughed. He was at the other side of the cell, backed by his coterie of toadies, Pinks, Moos, Brakes Peterson, Squinteye Samuels, Noor, and on the fringes of the gang, such satellites as Crip, Little Johnny, Solly and The Casbah Kid. They waited for the giant's reaction.

"Fair fight," Butcherboy laughed hoarsely, looking around at the faces of the onlookers. "The basket want a fair fight. Man to man."

And to his surprise there came a mutter from most voices, "Fair fight, fair fight." A murmur echoed even by his immediate henchmen. He peered about again. So it was like that, was it? He would have to get things in hand as soon as he had dealt with this big-mouthed skinny basket over there.

The battered face darkened and the stained and broken teeth were bared in a sneer. "Right," Butcherboy said. "Is a fair fight, hey." The hard round head turned on the thick neck and he ordered, "You, Brakes, stand by the door and listen when the guard comes around." He stared around at the others. "Clear this place and get over to the wall, all of you. And everybody stay quiet, understand? Not a sound. Dead still."

In a moment the crowd commenced pulling blankets and mats out of the way, piling them along the back wall of the caserne. That done, the spectators crowded onto the piled bedding or stood along the walls, everybody hushed and expectant, faces taut with excitement.

Butcherboy peeled off his shirt, and displayed the great torso, knotted with muscle and fat and cicatriced with old wounds, decorated with a gallery of tattooing. He flexed his biceps and slapped his chest, grinning with his bad teeth, displaying the pictures needled into his flesh: the skull-and-cross-bones, the flags and crossed daggers, the nude women who wiggled as his muscles writhed, and on the left side of the wide back, an eagle in full flight, its beak agape and wings spread, eyes glaring and talons hooked and poised for the kill.

He laughed cruelly, "Come on, *ou* pal, and let me squash you like a louse." His voice rumbled from his damaged larynx. "Fair fight, hey."

And now Yusef the Turk moved away from the wall where he had been leaning, and unbuttoned his shirt. In peg-topped trousers and brogues he appeared tubercular in comparison with the uncouth bulk of Butcherboy, but under the smooth, tan skin muscles rippled like lizards and the long body was really as tough and as flexible as a sjambok.

He put a hand to his mouth and slipped out his dentures. His face became thin and sunken. "Hold these for me, Professor," he said.

George Adams took the damp teeth, feeling somewhat ridiculous, and gingerly dropped them into a coat pocket.

Silence fell on the caserne in a dead weight. Over at the end of the room Butcherboy's henchmen waited, their eyes bright and evil in their treacherous faces. The Casbah Kid was as quiet and unemotional as a mummy, except that one eyelid twitched and narrowed as if winking slyly. Over by the iron-clad door, his ear to the judas-hole, the fried face of Brakes Peterson wore a fixed and ghastly grin.

Butcherboy shuffled forward. Below his stained khaki shorts, his legs were thick and ugly and knotted like tree-stumps. He growled, and as the sound rolled out of him, he thrust his huge right hand forward, as though to seize the other man in a wrestling hold.

With a lightning grab Yusef the Turk seized the extended hand, gave a swift jerk and released it before Butcherboy could free it and fasten upon him in turn. The swift tug upon his arm swung the giant half left and before he could recover his balance, Yusef the Turk drove at the side of his face with a chopping blow of the edge of his flat and rigid hand, laying open the flesh along the cheek-bone.

The spectators gasped and bodies grew stiff with tension as the giant reeled, and like the skilled master of innumerable street fights, Yusef the Turk gave him no chance to recover. The lean, plaited-leather body whirled sideways on the left foot while, at the same time, the right leg jerked up, knee high and then the foot shot out like a projectile, parallel with the floor. It caught the tottering Butcherboy in the belly with the force of a shell.

His eyes popped and a gust of breath belched from the gaping circle of his mouth with a sound like a hiccough. The knotted face worked as he gasped for breath, and the great body rocked like a boulder, but did not topple, and Yusef the Turk kicked him again, savagely, against the knee.

Butcherboy stumbled, his arms gyrating as he sought for balance. For years he had depended upon his size and ferocity to intimidate his victims; nobody lighter than he had ever attempted to challenge him to single combat, and the result was that now the swift onslaught of Yusef the Turk had both advantages of surprise and experience. Nevertheless, Butcherboy was only moderately hurt and shaken, and exasperated to the point of madness.

He roared and charged. Dodging clumsily under a swing, he reached out to fling his massive arms around the other's waist. As arms shot out for the deadly embrace, Yusef the Turk's knee flew up with terrific force to smash into the face so temptingly appearing above it. The face jerked aside in a flash, the knee missed it, and the leg was instantly seized in a grip like a vice. A sigh passed through the watchers.

But Yusef the Turk had been involved in too many fights of this kind. He snapped his left arm around Butcherboy's neck, getting it into the crook of the elbow, slipping the hand under his own right biceps, hooking it there. Then he slid the right forearm up and across the throat of his enemy, the side of the wrist against the Adam's apple, and with all his wiry strength he started to throttle the big man. Certainly, Butcherboy would throw him, but that would not free his throat from the garotte of sinew, bone and muscle that was relentlessly squeezing the air-pipe shut.

With a heave, Butcherboy threw Yusef the Turk and fell heavily on top of him. The latter's arms tightened, bone crushing the Adam's apple, and Yusef the Turk saw the face gradually turn blue, the tongue bulging. Swiftly Butcherboy changed his hold. Keeping one arm around the other's leg at the knee, he seized the foot with his other hand and drew it backwards with all his brute strength. As the leg bent backwards, he pressed the other arm tightly into the back of the knee. In a moment the leg would snap like a stick. Yusef the Turk knew it, and the sweat sprang like dew across his face, his eyes bulging from their sockets, toothless gums bared in a grunt of pain.

George Adams wanted to cry. He wanted to rush forward and kick the snarling face of Butcherboy to a pulp. Everybody waited, staring, for the sound of snapping bone.

Then Brakes Peterson, at the door, was hissing through the pregnant silence. "The guard. Here come the – – – – guard."

In a moment the antagonists parted, the spectators scrambled to the floor in positions of relaxation, looking at anything else but the door. Butcherboy slid flat, glaring at Yusef the Turk, his breath working like bellows. Yusef the Turk's face had assumed a greenish tinge under the tan skin, and his own lungs panted like those of a weary dog. His leg ached and he was worried about whether he would be able to use it against Butcherboy again. They were both slippery with sweat.

All heard the step of the guard in the yard outside. He was whistling as he went from peep-hole to peep-hole, and they could hear the tune of *Lili Marlene* through the crunch of his boots. The heat was soaked with silence inside the caserne, and when a man coughed suddenly, it sounded like the explosion of a faulty engine.

The whistling reached the cell door, and stopped. They heard the clink of the peep-hole cover being moved. Then a second clink as it fell back into place after the guard had looked in. The whistling started up again and moved away from the door, heading towards the gallery staircase.

"Brakes," asked Butcherboy, wheezing slightly, "Is it awright?"

"He's gone upstairs," the man with the burnt face said, sprawled at the foot of the door.

After a while the guard came downstairs again, and now he was whistling *It's a hap-hap-happy day*. They listened to him reach the foot of the stairs and then head down the yard towards the gate.

"Okay," Brakes said, and everybody sprang to their feet.

Butcherboy and Yusef the Turk rose to confront each other anew. The giant's split cheek-bone had swollen where Yusef the Turk's first blow had struck, and his eyes glared with a red and bloody light behind the pinched flesh of the lids.

Suddenly he charged. Yusef the Turk tried to sidestep the

onrush, but his painful knee slowed him up, and he felt the terrible arms close round his waist, pinioning his own arms at the same time.

The crowd buzzed with excitement, and Brakes Peterson snapped at them to shut up.

As the arms closed round him, Yusef the Turk butted Butcherboy's face savagely with his head, feeling the skin of his forehead split and a trickle of blood run into his eyes. But he also heard Butcherboy's grunt of pain as his head collided with the giant's nose, drawing a stream of blood that dribbled across the twisted upper lip into the snarling mouth and over the stubbled chin.

At the same time Yusef the Turk took the weight of his body quickly onto his weak leg and jerked the other knee brutally into Butcherboy's groin. The giant cried out with the sharp pain of the driving knee-bone, but held onto the other man, settling his head into Yusef the Turk's neck, while the powerful arms drew tight, squeezing with savage strength, the muscles twitching and jumping like cats in a sack.

Yusef the Turk knew that once he bent backwards there would be no hope. He would finally drop from the gorilla-like hug with a sprained or broken back, to receive smashing kicks in the face, ribs and stomach, before the giant jumped on him with both feet and all his hulking weight.

Butcherboy put all his force into the inward-drawing hug and his biceps and forearms swelled like balloons. Yusef the Turk, for a second, resisted with all his strength and then suddenly went limp, shooting his feet between the spread legs of his opponent and using his dead weight to bring both of them crashing to the ground. As Butcherboy came down on him, taken by surprise, Yusef the Turk had the time to jerk his head aside so that the other's bleeding face thumped into the concrete floor.

As Butcherboy's arms burst apart, Yusef the Turk squirmed swiftly from under him, striking at the cut cheek-bone and the neck with vicious chopping blows, scrambling to his feet. Butcherboy struggled ponderously upright, and before he could straighten, Yusef the Turk kicked him smartly in the solar plexus.

The honk as the wind was driven from Butcherboy's body was music to the ears of Yusef the Turk. He, himself, was breathing heavily now, and his back and knee pained, and he knew that he would not be able to last much longer against the stubborn strength of the big man. But he knew, too, that for seconds, with his wind gone, Butcherboy was at his mercy.

So, darting forward, he punched with left and right at the doubled-up, gasping giant, his arms jolting like piston-rods and his fists falling like hammer-blows on the bloody face. He felt the skin of his knuckles break under the force of the blows, driving the bulk ahead of him.

Butcherboy stumbled away, bellowing in a hoarse, breathless voice. He wanted to get away from the driving fists, so that he could re-group his disorganised defences. He reeled and half fell into the middle of his silent knot of henchmen and satellites, Moos, Pinks, Squinteye Samuels, The Casbah Kid, Noor, Solly, Little Johnny and the others. Against these he stumbled. Pinks and Noor put out their hands to stop him, Squinteye Samuels and Little Johnny closed to catch him, the others crowded forward in a pack, and The Casbah Kid's right hand jerked in a swift movement.

Butcherboy collapsed with a grunt, his thick legs suddenly flopping like rags, a look of amazement in the red glare of his eyes. Then the glare snapped out like a fused light and he slid to the ground in the middle of the milling throng.

He never moved or made a sound again. Somebody got a mug of water and splashed it over the bloody face, thinking that the hulk was merely unconscious. The whole cell crowded around, babbling. Somebody else turned Butcherboy over on his face. He lay big and limp and still, and a tiny fountain of blood was just slackening off into a thin trickle out of the eye of the tattooed eagle.

In another part of the crowd, The Casbah Kid's tongue flicked momentarily over his swollen lip.

PART II

1

The early evening lay purple in the square outside the Isolation Block, and a wind, little more than a breeze, had sprung up, making small blowing noises through the sprawl of buildings inside the walls of the prison. The leaking pipe was still dripping somewhere in the kitchen yard.

Everybody, except the boy who was called The Casbah Kid, and George Adams, had been served with the supper of bread and jam and coffee. Silence hung side by side with the evening over rows of stone cells with their iron doors and barred windows; over the Administration Block, dark now, over the entrance hall and the Reception. In the kitchen they were clearing up for the night – most of the squad had turned in because they came on duty again in the early hours of the morning. In the staff quarters, off-duty warders were getting ready to go out.

George Adams, sitting up against the wall, said to the boy opposite him, "You sleeping, mate?"

"No, man," The Casbah Kid said, his face to the wall.

"Listen, mate, I know you got troubles, but why did you have to go for that lighty there in the yard? I didn't see him do a thing to you, *mos*, mate."

The Casbah Kid said, without turning to look at him, "You's a helluva talker, mister. Talk, talk, talk. Okay, I will tell you. I hit the lighty because I wanted to be put over here."

"Here?" George Adams asked, frowning perplexedly.

The Casbah Kid said in his dry voice, "*Ja*, man. They going to *mos* ask questions about that Butcherboy, and I don't want to be around there when they ask, hey. Maybe they'll forget about us here, *mos*. I don't like talking about things. Maybe I seen things and I don't want to talk about it to the white men, see?" He added with a hint of suspicion in the flat tone, "You see a thing, mister? You was *mos* there, too."

George Adams said, looking at the boy's back: "Well, if they going to ask me if I saw anything, I'm just going to tell the truth. That's all, pal."

"Truth?" The Casbah Kid turned now, and still lying down, looked at George Adams.

"Yes, what," George Adams told him, pulling up a leg of his trousers and scratching his shin. "If they want *my* evidence, like. Man, I saw a fight between Butcherboy and Yusef, maybe is was a fair fight, maybe not, hey, but a fight with fists, man to man. Then I saw Yusef hit Butcherboy and he fell backwards into a crowd of other men who was watching, like. The next thing, Butcherboy collapsed, and when they turn him over – there, he's dead and somebody must have stuck him in the back with something. Who, I don't know. There was a lot of johns at that end of the cell. Yusef was in the middle of the cell and everybody else around the walls, *mos*. That's all." He pulled down the trouser leg and added, frowning, "Well, I'm kind of sorry for that poor basket, Butcherboy."

"Sorry?" The Casbah Kid sneered. "You? You're a funny *ou*, mister."

"I wonder how Yussy got on at the hospital. I heard they took him to get his back and knee X-rayed. And is funny, nobody can think what Butcherboy was stuck with."

"Turk isn't going to have anything to say," the boy said. He bit at a thumb and wiped it against his shirt. "I reckon he'll just tell them he fell down and hurt himself, *mos.*"

"*Ja,* I reckon so," George Adams said. He was about to say something further, but somebody in the cell next door began to thump on the party wall.

George Adams rose and went to the cell door. "Hullo," he called through the bars.

"Hullo, mate," the voice next door replied. "What for they put you here?"

"Talking back to Fatty," George Adams told the man. "He and the Major reckoned I'm making trouble."

"– – – – him," the other said. "That Fatty. Why they pull you in, mate?"

"Political," George Adams called back.

"Political?" the voice asked. "You mean you can go to jail for politics?"

"*Ja,*" George Adams laughed. "They reckon I'm planning to upset the government."

"*Ghod.*"

George Adams did not know which man was talking, but he remembered three of them exercising in the square, and when supper had been served, they had come upstairs and he had seen them again. They were all three serving convicts in the canvas shorts and red shirts of the Prisons Department.

"How you men keeping?" George Adams asked.

"Awright, man. Got to appear for further charges, hey." The man cleared his throat and went on: "Listen, mate, you got any tobacco?"

"Got some cigarettes."

"Right now this is a Non-Smoking Compartment, like," the other man said, laughing. "If you can spare some tobacco . . . ."

"We will see what we can do," George Adams told him. He turned away from the door and said to The Casbah Kid, "They need some tobacco. You reckon you can work it? You know *mos* the ropes."

"Blerry bum-slingers," The Casbah Kid said. "Always bumming. No *twak*, no this, no that."

"Well, they can't buy stuff like you can."

"You reckon I care?" the boy asked, looking sulky.

"No," George Adams told him, beginning to feel angry. "You don't give a – – – – for anybody. But I never heard you saying 'no' when you can get something given you for free. Don't I say?"

The boy looked at him sullenly. He said, "Well, we's in here together. I'd give you something, too, if I had it. What for you want to worry about *them*? They not with us, *mos*."

"Christ, everybody locked up behind bars here is with us," George Adams said.

"Blerry bum-hangers," The Casbah Kid said, his eyelid twitching as he gazed at George Adams. But he got up and rummaged in the pockets of his jeans until he found a little ball of cotton, while George Adams watched him curiously, feeling again like an immigrant in a strange country, ignorant of the habits and customs of its violent people.

"Give me a couple of cigarettes," the boy said in his bitter voice, his face as cold and expressionless as a window-pane.

He took the three cigarettes which George Adams handed to him from the box, and began to break them up into the palm of a hand. Then he found a scrap of brown wrapping-paper and made a tiny, flat parcel of tobacco. He folded the paper carefully, so that the package would not come apart, and then placing it on the floor, put a foot on it to flatten it wafer-thin.

George Adams said nothing, watching him and thinking, You poor sod, you poor, poor sod, you going to die and you don't give a damn about yourself and about anybody else; except maybe if you had been shown the way, and right now you're learning, even if it is too bloody late.

The fist thumped on the party wall again, and the man next door called, "You rerry, pal?"

"With you, mate," George Adams called back.

Now, unravelling the bunch of cotton until he had a long thread, The Casbah Kid went over to the door, at the same time taking a broken-off portion of a pocket comb from his jeans. He tied one end of the cotton to it. Next he tied the flat packet of tobacco carefully to the thread, a few feet from the comb, and crouched at the door.

"You watch the passage for the connection, mister," he said, looking at George Adams.

George Adams began to understand what was going to happen, and he chuckled, saying, "Well, I'll be damn'." He called, "You ready?" through the door.

"There's water. Let her go, chommy," the man next door replied.

The boy, crouching carefully out of the way of the cotton, suddenly shot the comb diagonally through the gap under the cell door, and George Adams saw it leap onto the balcony outside, dragging the cotton with it, and come to rest opposite the door of the other cell.

A moment later a button on the end of a thread of wool from an unravelled blanket, shot out from the cell and landed near the comb.

"Too short," George Adams said, watching through the bars and the mesh.

"We'll try again, mate," the convict said.

"Shoot her more to one side, our side," George Adams instructed, enjoying the newly discovered knowledge.

The button was withdrawn and then shot back in a moment. It came to rest with the wool across the boy's thread.

"Pull slowly," George Adams cried, feeling a twinge of excitement. "Slow, chommy, slow. So they will hook up. Ah, *hell*."

The button had missed the comb and was travelling back towards the other door.

The Casbah Kid shouted, "We'll both pull together, slowly, so they will hook up, hey."

"Right, mate," the voice, patient and unperturbed from long experience, replied.

The button snapped into sight once more, and crossed the thread. This time The Casbah Kid and the other man drew their threads simultaneously. George Adams watched the comb and the button slowly move towards each other.

"Slowly, slowly," he instructed from the window. "Slowly, hey, man. Hold it, hold it."

"What the hell now?" The Casbah Kid asked, and muttered a curse under his breath.

"Is okay," George Adams told him. "Only, just do it nice and slow, hey. Nice and slow."

The button and the broken comb, now about an inch apart, came gradually together, and then the button caught at the comb, the wool drawing it between the teeth, and the two threads were locked fast.

"Right-o," George Adams called. "Haul away."

"Right, pal," the man next door called. He began to gather in his thread, at the same time drawing the comb with it. The Casbah Kid paid out his cotton, and then slid the flat packet of tobacco under the door, and it was pulled slowly into the other cell. The convict there separated the comb and the button, called out again, and the boy drew back his cotton and retrieved the comb.

"Well," George Adams said, laughing. "That was a helluva trick. I would never have thought of it, pal. A helluva trick, that."

"Damn bum-slingers," The Casbah Kid said as he rolled up his ball of cotton.

George Adams laughed and slapped his back. Somewhere in the new darkness beyond them, the hymn-singer had started up again, solemnly, with *Jesus want me for a sunbeam* . . . .

2

At the sight of the dead body of Butcherboy, with its thin trickle of blood from the tiny hole in the back, just over the heart, the silence of shock had fallen upon the gaping crowd of prisoners. It had lasted for just a moment. Then there had been a general scramble for bedding. Mats and blankets were fought over as the men battled to spread their beds and be asleep, to disassociate themselves utterly from the incident before any further time passed.

In a few minutes they were huddled under smelly blankets, unconcerned about the sticky heat now. Nobody would say anything, except, if asked, that he had been asleep since the last bell had gone.

Certainly, one could think what one liked. Who had done it? Not Yusef the Turk, true as God. Towards the end of the fight – that had been a real wake-up scrap – he had been battering at Butcherboy's head with his fists. Not once did Butcherboy have his back to The Turk. And yet, somebody had stuck something into him, a knitting-needle or a nail or something. From behind. Well, he had been knocked flying into that gang of hard cases who followed him, Noor, Pinks, Moos, Little Johnny, Squinteye and others, and one of them, who had been awaiting a chance like this, had stabbed him in the back. But with what? Nobody knew, nobody could guess. There had been no sign of a weapon brandished. The white men would ask questions, make searches, but they would find nothing.

Butcherboy's former henchmen had performed certain last rites upon his body. They had washed his face, spread his mat and blankets, laid him out on the bed and had covered the lifeless gorilla body. These things they had done, not out of any respect for the dead monster, but for their own security.

One could not very well deny having seen a dead man sprawled out on the floor for an entire night, and not call the guard. When he came around again, he would look in and find the cell asleep, everybody under blankets. In the morning everybody would leave the cell at once, and when they checked later and found Butcherboy's corpse – well, how were they to prove that such and such a man had occupied the caserne that night. The authorities were only concerned with the exactness of their figures, not with what particular prisoner slept in what particular cell in the yard.

Yusef the Turk had limped over to the water urn and had washed blood and sweat from his face and torso. His forehead was cut, and one eye beginning to swell. Also, his right knee ached and the muscles of his back were lanced with sharp, twitching pain which came with each movement.

"What's going to happen now?" George Adams had whispered, coming up to him. "Here's your teeth."

"Nothing," Yusef the Turk said, wincing. He rinsed the dentures, inspected them briefly and slipped them into his mouth, clicking them to make them fit. "Nothing. Nobody is going to say a thing, Professor. When they open up in the morning, we all go out and leave it to the white men."

"But –" George Adams whispered, but Yusef the Turk had cut in, speaking angrily now.

"Listen, mate, this is a jail, see? This kind of thing happen now and then. They built this jail, so let them run it. The thing is, hey, that inside here people settle their own business and don't have nothing, or little, to do with the white man as possible. Now don't you go thinking this is like it is outside." He dabbed his eye with water. "Another thing, if you start to be a good boy and try to help the law, Butcherboy's pals isn't going to like it. One of them must've done it, and they won't like it talked about to the law. They's going to lay in the tracks of anybody what talks."

George Adams realised that Butcherboy's former gang, united, was as dangerous as Butcherboy had been alone, perhaps even more so. But nevertheless, he felt intimidated, and that irked him. He was feeling ill, too, and his stomach trembled like an old man's hand. He had never seen anybody murdered, and that and the fact that now he would have to spend a night in this cell, with a corpse lying nearby, horrified him.

He had swallowed the rush of saliva to his mouth, and had asked, "How you feeling, Yuss?"

Yusef the Turk sucked his skinned knuckles and scowled. "My head is not so bad. Is my back and the $----$ knee."

"You got to report sick in the morning."

"I reckon so."

"What you going to tell them?"

"$----$ all. I's sick, I's hurt. I fell down the stairs or something. That's all, man."

"They'll ask questions all over."

"Hell, I will worry about that when the time come. $----$ it."

Then he had limped back to where they had made a sleeping place for themselves, and George Adams had felt his stomach heave, and, unable to control it, had rushed over to the latrine bucket and had vomited.

Afterwards, he had lain awake for a long time, perspiring in the heat, unable to thrust from his mind the death of Butcherboy who had terrorised his fellows and then had fallen by the hand of one of them.

3

The man with the scar down the left side of his face rolled the long cigarette, tearing the brown paper carefully into a rectangle, working with the patient skill and care of a surgeon performing some delicate operation. He formed the strip of paper into a trench, holding it between thumb and third finger of one hand, the tip of the index finger in the hollow of the trench, keeping it in shape. With his other hand he shook the tobacco from the three cigarettes evenly along the length of the trench, arranged it smoothly with the tip of a calloused finger. When he was satisfied with the arrangement of the tobacco, he rolled the paper deftly into a tube, licked one edge and pasted it down and then licked the whole cylinder to make sure that the paper would stick, pinched each end and twisted them shut.

"Light," he said, inspecting the cigarette.

One of the other men in the cell pulled out his shirt and fiddled with the seam, and like a conjuror, produced half of a match which had been split carefully and expertly down the middle. The man with the scar took it, strolled to the wall and struck the match carefully on an exposed surface, cupping it quickly as the minute slice of sulphur flared. He puffed quickly at the handmade cigarette and then trickled smoke from his nostrils.

He went over to the door and looked out. Night hung over the prison like a purple shroud. The hymn-singer was silent. The man with the scarface came back, puffing with relish at the cigarette, and the man who had supplied the match, said: "You better fan that smoke away, Gus. That old guard come round and there's crack. You know *mos* we's not supposed to have *twak*."

"His backside," Gus said, and laughed, showing yellow teeth. When he smiled, the thin scar down the side of his face became jagged, forming a crooked white seam, as if it had been hurriedly sewn up with a faulty machine.

"He won't be here for a long time, man," he said.

"Maybe," the other man said. "But don't smoke the whole – – – – cigarette, hey."

"Okay, okay."

Gus smoked on and then looked at the burning end of the cigarette, blowing smoke at it. He was a thickset man of medium height, and had strong, thick legs, the calf-muscles over-developed and bulging like knotted hawsers under the skin. His feet were wide, the soles calloused.

He went over to where he had made his bed and sat down, folding his legs before him, like a fakir. He took two more puffs and then handed the cigarette to the man who had supplied the match.

This man had a very dark, flat, round face, like the bottom of a frying-pan on which somebody had, with a blunt finger-tip, hurriedly drawn eyes, nostrils and a heavy mouth in the layer of soot, burnt oil and congealed fat. When he spoke, he revealed incisors which protruded slightly, and a gold cap to one side of them. His eyes in the dark face were bright and brown, and full of humour.

He drew smoke into his lungs and grinned. "Long time since a man had some real tobacco. That's awright a john next door, hey." He smoked on and asked, "How long you reckon we going to pull for rushing that warder, *ou* Gus?"

Gus laughed. "Pull? What pull?" He was already serving an accumulated sentence of twenty-three years. He was twenty-seven years old, and he had no intention of finishing the sentence. He had started making arrangements for his escape, and now awaited the okay from friends outside.

He had purposely instigated an attack on a warder, drawing the dark man into it, because he did not want to make his intentions too obvious. The third man had joined the attack unexpectedly, suddenly appearing in the assault as if he had made up his mind on the spur of the moment. That part of the plan had worked all right, and they had been moved from the quarry prison to the city, as Gus had expected, to stand trial for assaulting the guard.

Gus, however, had not told the other two anything about his scheme. He would have to let them know at the last minute. They would be compelled to go with him – through the window onto the roof, anyway. After that they would have to take their chances on their own. They wouldn't stay behind, because they would be in further trouble for not sounding the alarm when he broke out, and he knew that they would go along, rather than do that.

Gus looked up at the rear window of the cell and smiled. It was covered with tough wire mesh on a framework inside, and outside was a row of four bars. Above was the parapet of the roof. He had been a cat burglar, and he had done a lot of wall-scaling and roof-climbing during his career.

Now he asked carelessly, "Pull? One year, two years, who cares?" He looked at the third man who sat on his blankets in a corner, arms embracing his knees, staring at nothing. "What's the matter with *him*?"

The dark man, whose name was Morgan, said, "Him? He's scared."

"Scared? A squash. A blerry fairy," Gus said, scowling at the man in the corner. This man was the youngest of the three, and now he was worried about the extra stretch which he faced for joining the attack on the guard. His eyes were dull, and his mouth curved sullenly downwards, a mark like the imprint of a horseshoe on his pale face.

He looked at the other two and said, "Leave me, men. I don't want to be worried, *mos*. Leave me."

"A blerry fairy," Gus sneered again. "I wonder what made him rush that guard with us. I wonder. You tell us, Koppe."

Koppe turned and said, talking on the verge of tears, "Hell, I didn't mean to, *mos*. It just happened, likely. Something made me to do it. I am going to tell that in court. I just saw you johns charge that special, and the next thing I was in it, too. I didn't *mean* to, hey. It was just something."

"So you didn't mean to, hey," Gus mocked him, imitating the other's voice. "You didn't *mean* to. But you's here, hey."

"Leave him, Gus," Morgan said. "Maybe he just went crazy, *bedonerd*."

"And now he's scared, hey? Fairy. I reckon he is only good for one blerry thing. Blerry fairy."

"Gus, leave me alone, Gus," Koppe pleaded, looking miserable. "Leave me alone, Gus."

"Ahh-hhh," Gus sneered.

He turned to Morgan, "Anybody downstairs in The Hole?"

"I didn't see nobody," Morgan said. He took a final puff at the diminished cigarette, and then held it out to Koppe.

"What for you want to give *that juba* a smoke?" Gus asked angrily.

"Hell, let him take a few drags," Morgan said.

Koppe took the butt from Morgan and muttered his thanks. His mouth worked nervously, and he was glad to have the cigarette-end with the harsh, burning brown paper between his lips. He smoked disconsolately, staring at the floor at his feet.

"No," Morgan said to Gus. "I didn't see nobody in The Hole."

Gus said, looking at Koppe, "Hey, squashy, how would you like to be locked up in The Hole?"

The Hole was on the ground floor; the punishment cell which was a square, windowless box, painted pitch black on the inside. Air came through a narrow, barred transom above the iron door, and that was the only opening in the stygian cell.

"I bet he will enjoy being locked up in The Hole," Gus went on, needling the frightened man. "Is dark inside there, and they say is haunted. Some john went mad and killed himself in there."

Koppe said nothing, but went on smoking. Gus stood up again and went over to him and jerked the last of the cigarette from his lips, and used up the few puffs which could still be dragged from it. He was irritable and impatient about making the break, like a pregnant woman near her time, and he projected all his bad humour on the frightened man in the corner.

Morgan said, "Siddown, Gus. Sit man. What's the matter, you got lice?"

Gus snorted and went surlily back to his blanket and lay down on it, folding his arms behind his head.

Morgan asked, "What those *jubas* in for next door?"

"One rooker is in for talking against the govvermen', like," Gus told him. "I think the other one chopped a man."

"Talking against the govvermen'," Morgan mused. "A man go to jail for almost anything nowadays, hey. Talking against the govvermen'. I'd like to do some talking against the – – – – govvermen'. *Ja*, a man go to jail for all kinds of things." He was lying on his back with his knees up and crossed, and he pointed with one bare foot at a conglomeration of scribbles on the wall opposite them.

"Look there now. See? *Toffy Williams*. There."

"Where?" Gus asked, looking.

"Right there, man. It say, *Toffy Williams Was Here For Murder.*"

"Oh, that. *Ja*, I see. What about it?"

"Because why, I knew *ou* Toffy. Talk about a man going up for anything. *He* was a unlucky basket, awright. Real bad luck, *ou* Toffy."

"What about him?" Gus asked. He was ready to listen to anything in order to rid himself of the feeling of impatience and frustration that had settled upon him.

Morgan shifted his back, settling down in what comfort the hard rope mat under the folded blanket on the concrete floor could provide. He said, "Well, is was like this":

Well, one night Toffy Williams was leaving the Duke's with his pal, Sam Niekerk. They'd had a few drinks and were on their way home. Now Toffy was a fisherman, working the trawlers, and went out to sea for days or weeks. You know how it is with fishermen. Well, every time he was due back, Sam would wait for him down at the Duke's near the docks, and they would have some drinks. Toffy earned a good screw, and extra when the catch was good, see? Sam was his pal, and he always treat old Sam to the drinks. Sam did some kind of a job in town, and he was free most of the time.

Anyway, they left this pub and was going along Dock Road, with Toffy carrying his gear over his shoulder, talking to each other, and they just turned a corner when something comes rushing along and right into Toffy, with such a bump that it almost knocks the gear flying.

'What the hell,' he cried, hanging onto his kit-bag.

'I'm sorry, mister,' a voice said breathlessly. It was a girl's voice, and looking down they found her clinging to the wall, trying to get up.

'Well, well,' said Toffy, laughing, and he helped her up. 'Did you get sore?'

'I's awright,' the girl said, laughing too.

Toffy looked at her. She was a nice piece to look at, all right. All painted up and soft hair; pretty as a doll.

Well, to cut a long story short, that was how Toffy met this Bella. The next thing you know, Toffy is going out with her, and although he still met his pal, Sam, at the Duke's whenever he came ashore, he did not have too much time for friends. Like it is when a man gets a girl. Sam, he thought she was just another Dock Road tart, but he did not say it to Toffy.

Some months went past, and Bella and Toffy were together every time he got home from a trip. Sam saw them off and on, apart from the times when he and Toffy met at the pub. They, Bella and Toffy, went to the bioscope or sat in the park or went to the beach when it was nice weather.

One evening they were sitting on a bench in the Public Gardens, and Bella, she seemed to be quiet. Toffy, he asked her what was the matter, and she said, 'Oh, nothing, man.' But he could see she had something on her mind, and he kept on asking until in the end she told him.

'I am going to have a child,' she said.

'There's water,' cried Toffy.

'What you going to do?' Bella asked.

'*Ek weet 'ie.* I don't know,' Toffy said awkwardly.

'I better have something done,' Bella told him.

'Done?' said Toffy. 'Where did you learn about that? You forget it, hey.'

'Must I then just have the child?' she asked him crossly.

'Naturally,' Toffy said. 'But we better get married.'

'You mean that, really?' Bella asked, happy now.

'Of course, man, baby. What you reckon?'

So they were married. They got a house from the ·Council, and Toffy had some money put away, so they could buy some furniture.

Sam Niekerk visited them now and then. Anyway, the child was born after a while, and it was a boy. It looked like Toffy, too.

Well, time went by, and Bella and Toffy seemed to get on all right. Naturally, they had their rows now and then, same as most married people, especially when Toffy was full of that old red.

One day Toffy came home from sea, and as usual went into the Duke's where Sam and others were hanging around.

'Hoit, men,' said Toffy, dropping his kit-bag at the foot of the bar.

'Hullo, Toff. How was the net?'

'Good catch this trip, pals,' Toffy said. 'Better make it a pint all round.'

'Better not spend all the chink,' Sam laughed. 'Missus will take the strap to you.'

Everybody laughed and Toffy said, 'Not that one. Love *ou* Toffy too much.'

Everybody laughed again and drank up. They all joked about Toffy being such a quiet, steady rooker since he got married, and how he paid up regularly to the wife when he got back from sea.

They had several rounds and things were going along happily.

'One thing,' somebody said, down the bar, 'Toff got something real nice to come home to. Nice and warm after the cold sea, hey.'

'You telling me,' said another.

'I reckon there's somebody else what think the same,' said a third, winking at others behind Toffy's head.

'What was that you said?' snapped Toffy, pushing his glass away.

'We know what we said,' a man laughed. 'Good *ou* Toffy.'

Toffy looked as dangerous as a shark, and stared at the others. 'What you baskets talking about?'

Then before they could answer, his pal, Sam, butted in and taking Toffy's arm, he said, 'Hear me, *ou* Toff. Come outside. We can talk there.'

'What's this?' Toffy asked, and picked up his gear, allowing Sam to lead him outside.

Outside, Sam said, 'What those johns mean is that all of us, we see this fruit-and-vegetable barrow standing outside your door mornings, and longer than it should, hey.'

'Whatter?'

'And this barrow boy is kind of a nice-looking john, too.'

Well, Toffy was in a rage. He could hear the others laughing merrily inside the pub. He was a simple sort of a john, and didn't like any nonsense. But it was already late in the morning, and when he thought it over, he decided that he would not go home right then. He would go home the next morning, early.

So he left Sam and spent the rest of the day in other pubs and most of that night in a shebeen, trying to drown the doubt and suspicion that gnawed at him inside, like a rat at a roll of cheese.

The next morning old Toffy walked unsteadily to his home. *Bedonerd,* a lot of – – – – foolish baskets, those men. And that Sam, too. He ought to know better than to tell tales about a pal's wife, like that. Nice and warm to come home to after the cold sea. There's somebody else what thinks the same. Trying to be funny with him. Give him a fright, likely. But he knew when he had a good thing . . . .

He came into his street and his drugged eyes widened. There *was* the barrow, half-laden with greens outside his house, and the front door shut.

Toffy stood there, staring at the evidence. Nice and warm to come home to. Kind of a nice-looking john, too.

Before he knew what he was doing, he was inside the house. His fish-knife gleamed like a white-hot flame. Bella screeched. The barrow man looked shocked to see him.

Bella, she had little to say to the court. She had asked the barrow man to carry her purchases into the house for her, and he had done so, as he always did.

"*Ja*," said Morgan, smiling with his big teeth. "A man can go up for all kind of things. Some say it was Toffy's fault for taking up with a goose he pick up on Dock Road. I don't know, hey."

"And what happen to this Bella?" Gus asked, turning on his side to face Morgan.

The dark man yawned loudly and scratched his chest through his faded red shirt. "Ahh-hhh," he said. "She took up with that Sam Niekerk soon after."

4

The night-guard had come and gone. They had heard the door downstairs being unbolted, shortly after the last bell had rung, and the sound of his boots on the concrete steps as he came upstairs. He had paused at each of the two occupied cells in the Isolation Block, to rattle the bars in the doors and to look in. George Adams, stretched out on his blanket, had seen the guard's face and uniform cap dissected into rectangles and small squares by the bars and the screen, like the parts of a puzzle fitted together. Then they had heard his footsteps going downstairs, the iron door below being slammed and locked again.

Locking and unlocking, George Adams thought. All these birds do is lock and unlock. It must be great exercise for the mind. It occurred to him that all guards in a prison were practically prisoners themselves, that they lived most of their working life behind stone walls and bars; they were manacled to the other end of the chain.

He yawned, wondering what had happened to Yusef the Turk, and what would come of this whole business.

Everybody had made a rush for the door as soon as it

had been opened that morning, and were out into the yard, struggling into their clothes, with Butcherboy, his heavy bulk looking as if he was still asleep, under the blankets.

Yusef the Turk had pushed George Adams ahead, while the latter protested half-heartedly, and out in the yard George Adams had said, "Christ, we's just not going to *leave* him there, man."

"What the hell you want to do, man – *carry* him?" Yusef the Turk had hissed. "You just go about things ordinary, like, pal. Leave everything to these other baskets. They know what to say and do."

And George Adams had felt infinitely sad all of a sudden, as if he was abandoning the body of a friend during a retreat.

Later, when everybody had formed up, there had been consternation among the guards who were counting off the prisoners, because they discovered one short. They had counted twice, and then one of them had gone from cell to cell, until he had come across the body of Butcherboy.

This warder had come back, shouting excitedly, "Hey, there's one of them dead in here." Fatty and another guard who was about to go off duty, went into the cell. Then all three of them had come out again and Fatty had faced the assembled prisoners, his plump red face cold and suspicious in the early light.

"Who of you men slept in that cell last night? Step out."

And the column of prisoners had stirred and shuffled, but nobody said a word and nobody stepped forward. Fatty had laughed a cold laugh, and had looked at the other guards.

"Of course, nobody slept in there. None of these baskets will know a thing."

"I'm going to rouse the Super," one of the other guards had said.

"Awright, mate. Go ahead."

That guard had gone off and Fatty had walked slowly down the length of the column, his eyes as chill and rigid as death, watching each face in turn, while the mouth grinned mirthlessly under the pale blonde moustache.

After a while the Superintendent had arrived, long and thin and bony, walking with his head thrust forward on his leathery neck, like a beagle on the scent.

That was when the boy called The Casbah Kid had started the rumpus. There was a shout, the column broke, the men at the centre of the disturbance scattering, and there was The Casbah Kid, with a metal mug strung on a belt, lashing at another boy with it, the mug banging into the head and shoulders while the victim cowered, crying out in pain as he tried to protect his face.

The guards had rushed into the melee, snapping orders, thrusting men aside, and Fatty had grabbed the boy by the collar of his shirt and flung him away, wrenching the improvised weapon from him as he did so. The Superintendent looked furious and marched up to The Casbah Kid, his long legs working like the limbs of some contraption.

"What the hell is the matter with you?" he had shouted, holding his swagger-stick like a club.

The Casbah Kid straightened to his feet and looked surly, but said nothing, his teeth kneading his lower lip and his eyes somewhere in the distance.

"Who is this one?" asked the Super, and the fat guard said to the boy, "Show the boss your card, bogger."

The Casbah Kid dragged his ID card from a pocket of his jeans, and not looking at Fatty, held it up. The Super looked at it and snorted. "Another bloody knife stabber, I suppose. Hard case, hey?" He nodded slowly, and with his long neck, he had the appearance of a mechanical toy which moved the head when wound up. "Three meals off and segregation," he snapped. "Until further notice." He eyed the fat guard again and Fatty saluted.

"Come on you," he had ordered The Casbah Kid, and poked him with the end of his truncheon.

"I wonder what for that *bedonerde* fool done that," Yusef the Turk had muttered, rubbing his back where the pain twitched.

"You better report sick," George Adams had told him.

"Not now. These johns not going to listen to no complaints now, anyway."

While they were talking, two convicts came up carrying a stretcher between them, and accompanied by the sick-bay orderly who wore a white coat over his uniform. Then all of them, the Super, the guards, the stretcher-bearers and the orderly, went into the cell.

The prisoners waited in their lines, starting to talk in mutters, looking about, and George Adams saw Butcherboy's former henchmen standing together, Moos, Noor, Little Johnny, Brakes Peterson, Squinteye and Pinks, all grinning and whispering. I wonder which one of that lot did it, George Adams thought. Every one of them looks mean enough to pinch his grandmother's teeth while she sneezed.

Then the sick-bay orderly came out, followed by the convicts carrying Butcherboy's body under his blanket on the stretcher, and then the Super with the guards trailing behind.

The Super was saying, ". . . . they treat this prison like it was a damned bar-room." He stared at the lines of prisoners who had now fallen silent. He was angry and also worried. The Prisons Department expected him to keep proper order and to run the prison without its internal demerits being exposed too much. Prisons had a bad enough reputation, and he was wondering how he was going to be able to prevent any explosion over this matter. He went towards the gate looking sour and harassed.

Later on the breakfast of porridge had been served and eaten in silence. The stillness seemed to worry the fat guard and he had patrolled the yard slowly, the bunch of keys dangling from one hand clink-clinking through the silence that was like a part of the sunlight and the patterns of shadows on the stone walls.

When breakfast was over, Yusef the Turk had risen awkwardly, and winking at George Adams, had limped over towards the guard. George Adams and others had watched them talking together, had seen the guard's look of suspicion. He had said something and looked Yusef the Turk up and

down, and then had said something again, gesticulating with
the bunch of keys, and Yusef the Turk had pointed at his
back and at his knee, speaking all the time, and the guard
had shaken his head and said a word which must have been
a curse. Then he had gone over to the gate and had unlocked
it, passing Yusef the Turk over to the guard who watched in
the square outside the grille. Yusef the Turk had gone down
the square towards the archway to the sick-bay with the
guard, and that had been the last George Adams had seen
of him that day.

While the prisoners set about cleaning up the yard, sweeping the cells and emptying the night-soil buckets, things had
returned gradually to normal and conversation developed,
so that once more the yard hummed with the murmur of
voices.

The fat guard continued to patrol the yard, and everybody
guessed that he was hoping to pick up some information
about Butcherboy's death, but the muttering broke off whenever he drew near, to be resumed when he had passed, and
he had gone on, looking cold and angry.

George Adams had been standing in a wedge of shade
when the prison cat had stepped delicately over his feet, and
he had stooped and picked up the cat, smiling at it and
running his hand down the silky back, watching the fur rise
as his hand passed. The cat had purred and had licked his
wrist, the tongue warm and rough.

Somebody had said, "What business you got with that
cat?" And looking up, there was Fatty staring at him with
his wintry eyes.

"Oh, I was just playing with it," George Adams had said
mildly.

"Playing? You think you here to play?"

"There's nothing wrong in picking up the cat," George
Adams had replied, purposely keeping his tone nonchalant.

"Still talking back, hey? Still a blerry *slim* bogger."

"You asked me a question, so I answered," George Adams
had said. He wanted to laugh at the guard's harassment and

110

consternation, thinking, This lot really got old Fatso by the short hairs; he's nervous as hell.

"I've had enough of your cheek," the guard snapped at him, waving a finger like a pink, smoked sausage under his nose. "You'll see who's clever here. Now put that cat down and come with me. We'll see."

George Adams had put the cat down and had smiled thinly through the stubble that charred his face. He went after the fat man, and a laugh had gone up as the prisoners watched the guard's angry, jiggling walk. He looked like a plump woman hurrying off to keep an appointment.

The guard had unlocked the gate and had motioned George Adams through into the square. "All right, you stand there until the Major comes around," Fatty had said. To the guard in the square he had said: "Keep an eye on this *bliksem*, mate."

George Adams had stood in the sun, outside the grille, for a long time, watching the convicts, three of them from the Isolation Block, taking their exercise, plodding round and round in circles. One of the convicts had a thin knife-scar down the side of his face, and another was very dark. The third looked worried and had a slight, worn-out body. Their bare feet went slap-slap, slap-slap on the asphalt of the square as they circled again and again. The sun was hot in the square and after a while they were all sweating.

Later in the morning a warder came out of the Headquarters Block and hammered on the iron triangle hanging outside the door, and the guards shouted, "Fall in, fall in."

In the yard the prisoners were lining up and silence fell again. Standing alone in the glare of the sun, George Adams felt sleepy, and wished he could have lain down.

The prison cat came through the bars of the grille into the square and headed towards the kitchen behind the Isolation Block, and he watched it sleepily, thinking, Kitty, kitty, nice kitty, you got me into trouble, kitty.

Then the Superintendent had come into the yard and had headed, first towards the white section next door, and

George Adams had watched him go, tall and knobbly, the lank body leaning forward a little from the waist, looking like a scarecrow about to topple over. He carried his swagger-stick clenched under one arm, and he looked angry.

When he had inspected the white prisoners he headed for the Coloured Remand Section, and stopping by George Adams, he had said, "Well, what's this?"

The fat guard who had come out of the Remand yard, saluted and said, "This one has been giving lots of trouble, Major. A cheeky one who thinks he's clever. Always talking back, Major." To George Adams he had said harshly, "Your card, *jong*."

The Super had looked at the card and his face had grown angrier still. He had said, "Hmmm. *Ja*, one of *those*. Illegal organisation, hey." He stared at George Adams, the crumpled pink face suffused. "I've had enough nonsense, do you hear? I've had enough nonsense. There's enough trouble in this section. Look what happened here last night. I've had enough. You people think this is a public meeting. Stirring up trouble." He had said to the fat guard: "Meals off for the rest of the day, and transfer him to the Isolation Block." Then he had gone off into the yard, saying, "Nobody knows a thing about it, of course. Not a thing . . . ."

Now, lying in the cell, with The Casbah Kid in the other corner, George Adams, drifting into sleep, heard the wind coming up. The wind made whistling sounds through the prison, soaring down passages and through the deserted yards, leaning against the stone walls and turning away in frustration, cooing plaintively, plucking irritably at eaves and doorways. During the night it would grow stronger and howl in rage at the immovable obstruction of the stone, tear at gates and bars, pound the concrete and brownstone, thrust futilely at walls and then growl on its way over the city.

Through the sound of the rising wind, the hesitant drip-drip of the unseen water-pipe played a reluctant counterpoint, and George Adams dreamed that he was in the backyard of the house where he lived, and Butcherboy was saying, "Somebody got to fix that tap." Butcherboy had a bundle of pamphlets under an arm and he said to George Adams, "We got to hand this out by tonight before they lock us in." "You can get Jefferson and Yussy to help you," George Adams told him. "I've got to cut that Yussy's blerry throat." Then there was Butcherboy being carried away on a stretcher, holding the bundle of pamphlets, saying, "Who killed cock robin?" And then Mrs. Isaacs, the landlady, was saying, "I've had enough nonsense. You'll hang by the neck until you're dead, dead, dead. Come on, wake up now, here's your tea." She was holding a bowl full of beans and she shook George Adams with her free hand, calling, "Come on, you'll be late for work. Up, up, up."

George Adams woke up, saying, "Whatter?" And there was The Casbah Kid, gripping his shoulder and shaking him. "Time to get up, mister. The bell went awready."

The wind had died away, and the early summer sun, splashing through the back window, made a stippled pattern of mesh-work on the floor.

5

Slup-slup. Slup-slup.

Round and round the circle moved, the bare feet of the three convicts slapping the hot tarmac of the square. Behind them walked The Casbah Kid and George Adams. Obliquely above them the sun hung like a red-hot coin in the sky. Although a canopy of wind cloud lay motionless along the top of the mountain, there was not a breeze moving in the late-morning air.

Slup-slup. Slup-slup.

The wheel of walking men went round and round, their shadows trailing like black rags tied to their feet, sweeping the sunlight before them. In the shade of the wall of the Isolation Block the guard stood, looking bored. Behind the high steel grille the prisoners in the Remand yard sat in stolid rows with the sun encroaching inexorably on the shade where they were gathered as they waited for the next clang of the triangle which would announce lunch.

A head warder passed through the square and the fat guard in the yard shouted, "Caps off, caps off." A clerk went through, carrying a thick book, and joked with the guard in the shade. In the kitchen, pot-lids clanged and the leaking pipe still dribbled monotonously with its tantalising invitation to ice-cold water.

Slap-slap. Slap-slap.

In front of George Adams was the slight back of The Casbah Kid, his jeans sagging loosely, the rubber-soled gym shoes, worn and dirty, imitating the sounds of the bare feet of the convicts ahead. He plodded with obstinate stolidity, wrapped up in his own personal armour of silence, hiding his secret thoughts under invisible layers of dispassionate blankness.

Behind him, George Adams thought, This is one way of losing weight. He was perspiring under his shirt, and wondered what would happen if he dropped out to rest. Rounding the areaway in which they marched, he smiled at the dark, flat-faced convict as he passed opposite him, and the face split into a gold-toothed grin, and eyelid winking. Earlier, when they had all been ordered downstairs, the man with the knife-scar had thanked him for the tobacco, and George Adams had thought them a friendly enough pair. The third man looked sullen and had not said anything.

Slap-slap. Slap-slap.

The five of them tramped round and round. Gus was watching the yard, looking out for somebody behind the grille, the man who would give him the sign that everything was arranged. Walking round and round in the sun, his eyes, narrowed against the sharp light, searched the lines of prisoners who sat muttering in the yard. But the man he sought took no notice of him, and he tramped on, thinking, I hope those baskets got everything fixed up; they better have everything fixed up.

Slap-slap. Slap-slap.

A safari of hard-labour convicts emerged from the direction of the stores, and George Adams looked in astonishment at them, for each man was laden with a huge bag of ground meal, carrying it on neck and shoulders, bare legs quivering and straining under the impossible weight. Bowed like so many Atlases, each supporting his Earth, they toiled shakily towards the kitchen, muscles knotted painfully and faces suffused.

Now a Coloured warder came into the square, up to the grille of the Remand Section and started calling names from a list. One by one the prisoners came forward and were let out through the gate. George Adams heard his own name, and he signalled to the guard in the shade, and fell out to join the others.

Among the group was the little man, Solly, who grinned at him, cackling, "*Hoit*, pally. So they give you a separate room, hey?"

"*Ja*," George Adams laughed. "Grand Hotel. What happened in here?"

"Law came yesterday afternoon," Solly said. He was gazing past George Adams with wrinkled eyes, trying to catch the attention of Gus who was plodding mechanically around the square. "Nobody said nothing," he went on, grinning, but not looking at George Adams. "They will go on asking things out, reckon and think. Maybe some fairy will talk, or maybe they will give up." He shrugged, then he caught Gus's eye and raised his hand slightly in an obscure signal and Gus winked at him, nodding his head. Gus went on around the square, grinning secretly to himself.

The warder went through the names and then ordered everybody to fall in in twos and they all trooped after him, towards the visitor's gate.

Next to the outer grille, where George Adams had collected his parcel, was a door in the wall, and now the warder opened it and counted off six of them into the cage beyond. The cage was wide enough to hold six at a time, standing in a row. In front of them was a wire screen reaching to the ceiling and opposite that, about four feet away, another screen behind which the visitors had to stand.

Standing there behind the wire, George Adams felt a ripple of excitement like a current of electricity. His heart beat like a gavel and he wondered who was coming to see him; whether it was one of the committee or a friend. And he almost cried out with pleasure, for there was Mrs. Isaacs, his landlady.

Small and lean, she looked a little nervous and apprehensive, and at the same time she felt indignant at having to visit somebody in a prison. George was a nice, respectable boy, she thought, even though he mixed up with funny people who went around talking against the government. One left the authorities alone and let them do what they pleased; God would see to everything in the end. But if they had to arrest George for such things, at least they could keep him in some special place, instead of among all these thieves, hooligans and good-for-nothings. Now, seeing George Adams with his face scorched with stubble and his eyes somewhat red-rimmed, a lump jumped into her throat and she felt for a handkerchief in order to dab away a tear.

George Adams, in turn, smiled and waved to her across the intervening space, saying, "Why, Missus Isaacs, it is nice to see you. And for you to take the trouble of coming up here."

She had put on her Sunday best; he recognised the pink coat and the black straw hat with gay, imitation flowers around the crown.

There were other women and men in the visitor's cage and when all tried to talk together, they found it difficult to hear, so in a moment everybody raised their voices, gesticulating across the cage in a mixture of words and sign-language.

"Are you awright?" called Mrs. Isaacs, standing next to a vast, jiggling woman in a gaudy dress as big as a beach tent, and fat hands like blown-up rubber gloves, decorated with cheap Woolworth jewellery, who happened to be visiting the clownish little man, Solly.

"Fine, fine," George Adams cried through the babble of other voices.

". . . . Sunday," the fat woman bellowed.

"You need a shave," shouted Mrs. Isaacs and glanced crossly at the woman.

"They only take orders next Tuesday," George Adams called. "I got to buy blades. None allowed in."

"Tell him for Sunday," the fat woman yelled. She was perspiring and the powder on her face was turning to paste and starting to run.

Somebody else was shouting, ". . . . the bail money."

"Your committee gave me some things for you," Mrs. Isaacs called to George Adams. "I handed it in. Did you get the other stuff on Wednesday?"

"Thanks."

". . . . a car," the fat woman cried. "Up there, that street." She gestured with a blown-up hand towards the east. "Sunday night. I handed in some nice things for you, Solly." She winked broadly at him.

"Safe, aunty, safe," Solly yelled back, and cackled with laughter.

Another voice yelled: "Did you bring . . . ."

"They also paid your back rent," Mrs. Isaacs cried and looked jokingly stern. George Adams laughed and waved to her, blew a kiss and yelled, "I dreamed about you last night. You're my favourite girl." Mrs. Isaacs laughed and showed bare upper gums.

"You tell him is fix up," the fat woman bawled.

"Fix up, fix up," Solly piped back, winking.

"Your lawyer will come see you on Monday or Tuesday," Mrs. Isaacs cried, cupping a hand to her mouth.

"Thanks, thanks."

"Tell him not to worry, hey."

"I will. Fix up, fix up, *mos*."

"I brought your khaki shirt, George. You better send that

one out for washing. And your socks. I handed in socks and a handkerchief. You need anything more?"

Everybody yelled back and forth, continuing the pandemonium in the cage. It went on until the guard rang a bell several times, and the visitors had to leave. Mrs. Isaacs fluttered her hand and George Adams waved to her. The fat woman winked again at Solly and said good-bye, and went out of the cage, swaying like an elephant. Everybody waved and called greetings through the wire.

6

"How the hell we going to open these peaches?" George Adams asked.

"You can ask the guard for a tin-opener," The Casbah Kid said. "They got one in the store next door."

"Oh. I'll ask him. Well, we can have canned peaches, and here's a tin of stewed steak. Four apples, a packet of toffees and cigarettes."

"Never seen steak in tins," the boy said. He entertained a suspicion that he was being trapped by the other man's hospitality, and he spoke with reluctance.

"So we can have a picnic, man," George Adams laughed.

"Go on, mister."

"Well, we got our dinner bowls and we won't hand them in until tomorrow. Keep them for this stuff in the tins."

"I don't want to do you short, mister. I reckon your people brought it for you, *mos*."

"*Garn*. That's awright, mate. Enough for' two."

"T'anks, mister." Appreciation was strange in the boy's mouth, like the taste of medicine.

"Here, have a cigarette, mate. Help yourself, chommy."

"You's funny people, mister." The child-face with the ancient, bitter eyes, frowned. "Hear me, mister. All this stuff about our people getting into the government, too. You reckon it will help people like us? People in prison, like?"

George Adams said to this strange boy who was also a murderer: "There will certainly be more sympathy, I reckon."

"You reckon that time will come?"

George Adams said, feeling sad: "You'll see."

7

That basket, Solly, must have seen somebody today, Gus thought, staring at the ceiling of the cell from the blanket on which he relaxed. They must have sent somebody about this business. Maybe Willy, or *ou* Baard. Maybe is was Uncle Koos or even that fat Florrie.

He was excited and impatient now that he knew definitely that the wheels were still moving. They had sent Solly in on some minor charge, of course, once they knew that he, Gus, was being moved to this prison. Gus thought about Koppe. That basket is scared, the fairy. He might muck up the whole blerry business. But he would not know about it until the last minute, anyway. Once Gus was out through the window, it would be easy. Over walls and roofs, that was a small matter. He knew about climbing buildings.

. . . . He slid around to the sheltered side of the parapet, while the rain lashed at him like whips, stinging with iciness. Down the street, a block of flats blazed like a huge illuminated Christmas tree in the dripping darkness. A car went up the street below him, a black bug under the rain. The roof sloped dangerously upwards to a ridge, wet and slippery. The rain beat against his face and ran down into his neck. He went up the slope, moving expertly over the wet corrugated metal, straddled the ridge for a moment to stare into the darkness for any sign of watchers. But there was only the rain and the sparse forest of chimneys, outlet pipes and wind-vanes around him. Down the other side, and there was no brick parapet this time, but a narrow gutter running along the edge of the roof. Once his foot slipped and he slithered over the dribbling metal

of the sloping roof, and, for a moment, the spike of an electric standard speared upwards at him, menacing as a sword-fish out of the sea of rain. But his strong fingers saved him and his feet found the gutter and reached the top of a drain-pipe, and then he was climbing slowly, carefully, wetly downwards towards the window below ....

No, they would not catch *him*, not *ou* Gus. He was an expert at his job.

8

With his chicken-claw hands, Solly examined the contents of the paper carrier which the fat woman had sent in to him. He chuckled gleefully. There were two tins of fish in tomato sauce, a packet of twenty cigarettes, three bananas and a large loaf of bread which the inspectors had slit lengthways down the middle. Without removing the groceries from the packet, he examined them.

From the other side of the cell, Brakes Peterson called with a gargoyle grin, "You got something nice there for us, Solly?"

"Nice, nice. Nice things, pally," Solly cackled. He broke off a banana and tossed it across to the man with the burnt face.

He examined the loaf. At one end, near its base, well below the cut which the inspectors had made, was a thin, narrow slit, almost invisible. He stuck a thumb with a long, black nail into the slit, tearing the crust away, and drew forth three new hack-saw blades. Careful not to expose them, he rolled the blades in a sheet of newspaper in which the bananas and cigarettes had been wrapped, and disguised the long packet into what looked like a rough twist of scrap paper. He laid it in the bottom of the carrier with the cigarettes, the bread and the tinned fish, turned the carrier into a parcel and stowed it away under his blanket roll. Then he began to peel a banana.

9

On Saturday mornings there was usually a bustle in the section. The guards on duty went off soon after the last meal was served, and so breakfast, lunch and supper for the prisoners were all squeezed into that one morning. It did not occur to the authorities that there was anything wrong in leaving a man locked up from shortly after noon until the next morning without a meal.

The guards were impatient after they unlocked in the morning. They were all thinking about the cricket match that day, or going for a drive with their families, or just lazing away the week-end. So they hurried the prisoners, snapping orders, calling to the kitchen staff to pull finger with the breakfast mush.

Solly woke up with the first stroke of the bell. He woke up immediately, like an animal scenting the presence of an enemy, and looked about. One wrinkled hand slid under the folded blanket he used as a pillow, and made certain that his parcel was still there. He did not think that anybody could have handled it during the night without waking him, but he made sure.

All over, bodies were stirring, struggling out of sleep in the pale light of the summer morning. The air was stale and heavy with the smell of perspiration and musty blankets. Outside, the wind had been blowing all night, and now was dropping with gasping sighs, like an old woman on her death-bed.

Then Solly was up, pulling on his stained shorts and stuffing his long shirt into them, calling jokingly: "Wakie, wakie, babies. Time for your nice morning porridge, children. Can't keep *ou* Major Planks waiting, hey."

Around him, men groaned and cursed, yawning, rubbing the night from their eyes, looking dull and stupefied.

"Up, shake up," cried Solly, performing his travesty of a ballet. He was eager to get going with his part of the escape plan, and his eyes, bright as polished shoe-buttons, were urgent in the dry folds and wrinkles of his face.

"Lord," somebody growled. "You *mos* full of sparks today, *ou* Solly."

"Sparks, sparks, what sparks," Solly piped. "I'm not a blerry lazy-bones like you *jubas*. Listen, when I was on the farm, we use to get up two o'clock to drive the cattle, reckon and think. Sparks, sparks."

He started to fold his own blankets, saying, "Saturday today. We all going to the big match this afternoon." He laughed foolishly. "You johns better hurry up. I want to clean up here."

"*You* clean up? It never happen before, *ou* Solly," another man laughed.

The prisoners were all up now, shaking out blankets and folding them, rolling up mats. Brakes Peterson, Noor, Squint-eye and others of that clique had already bullied a few lesser elements into doing their chores for them every morning, so they were standing around, lighting cigarettes and talking through yawns. With the passing of Butcherboy they had automatically moved into a position of ruling body. It now remained to be seen which single one of them would emerge as a dictator, would have the initiative to launch a sort of palace revolution.

"Say, *ou* Solly," Squinteye said. "You see we get some hot water this morning, hey. We want to make some cocoa. Never had a cuppy cocoa for days." He looked about with his good eye. "Where's that basket with that tin of cocoa?"

"Hot water, *me*?" Solly sneered at him. "You reckon *I* got to carry hot water for *you*? Hey, you reckon I'm a blerry butler?" He spat. "You find yourself a servant girl, pally."

Squinteye scratched himself and laughed. "Awright, awright, don't get on your little horse, pal. I was testing you, like." They did not bully the little man; he had assumed the position of court jester.

"Testing," Solly said. "I wish they'd open up. I want to sweep out this place."

But first they had to fall in to be counted, and then breakfast was issued, and only after breakfast, when the whole section set about cleaning up the yard and the cells, was he able to get back to his own cell.

A squad of prisoners carried away the night-soil buckets, and the water urns for refilling. Solly attacked the floor with a broom, sweeping it quickly and cleanly, because he did not want to arouse any possible suspicion by leaving the task half-done after his initial display of enthusiasm.

He was worried, however. He had to get the saw-blades to Gus, and the guards and other authorities were very strict about preventing communications between convicts and prisoners still awaiting trial.

So that, now, piling all the detritus of confinement – cigarette butts, scraps of paper, orange peels, sardine cans, blanket fluff, match ends – into a bucket, he wondered how he would manage to contact Gus. His creaking, dusty brain, rickety as an old chair, was incapable of any elaborate planning, and for a while he was angry with himself for having volunteered for this duty. Now that the climax of the plan was approaching, his usual exuberance began to falter like a clogged motor, and he felt as deflated as a punctured balloon.

Muttering to himself, he went back to his blanket roll, unpacked the paper carrier, and took out the long twist of newspaper containing the blades. He placed this inconspicuously on top of the rubbish in the bucket, stowed his parcel away again, and then carrying the bucket before him like a votive offering, he left the cell.

He went down the wet yard which the prisoners were splashing and scrubbing, oblivious of the water being dashed over his gnarled feet. The bins for the sweepings of the section were against the grille, outside the gate, and prisoners from other cells were passing in and out through the gate which had been unlocked, carrying their buckets.

To one side of the gate, away from the bins, a crowd of idling men had gathered to watch something in the square.

Through the bars of the grille, Solly could see the prisoners from the Isolation Block: The Casbah Kid, that strange, short man who seemed to be everybody's friend, and the convict with the dark face, and the younger one, and Gus. Near them stood Fatty, with the guard who did duty in the square, and the one from the white section.

Solly went down the yard, and looking up, Gus saw him, and Solly nodded across the distance, still wondering how Gus would reach him. Then when he reached the gate, he saw what was happening in the square.

10

The prison cat had caught a mouse and was in the process of worrying it to death before devouring it.

The mouse, small and grey, had no intention of being devoured, but there, in the hot glare of the sun that practically blinded it, and dizzy from the blows it had received from the cat's great paw, there seemed little hope. Standing splay-legged in the sunlight, it now watched the great blur that was the cat. The tiny lungs of the mouse panted as it strained for breath. It stood with its bluntly-pointed head up, ears cocked and tail limp on the hot asphalt, the dusty-grey body throbbing.

Suddenly it attempted a dash sideways, the body darting through the sunlight, but the cat clubbed it casually and it spun away and then tumbled over and over, and the cat followed it swiftly, fur rippling and tail swishing, and clubbed it again with the balled paw.

The three guards were watching, with fascination, the punishment of the mouse, chuckling, as if they felt a natural association with the feline sadism. Behind the grille, a crowd of prisoners also watched.

And Gus, seeing the attention of the guards distracted, started to saunter slowly past their backs towards the grille. He picked up a scrap of paper and a peel which somebody had dropped, and held it ostentatiously, so that anybody who happened to look his way would see nothing suspicious in his movement to the bins.

The cat lay on its belly, forepaws extended, watching the dazed mouse with cruel, glowing, yellow-green eyes. The curved, predatory claws stretched menacingly from under the fur of its paws, ready to strike. In the eyes of the spectators, it appeared bored and lazy, but its whole body was tensed, alert, waiting for the next move of the mouse. The head of the mouse twitched, darting from side to side, looking for refuge. There was a tiny streak of blood on its mouth.

Solly strolled through the gate into the square and turned right, towards the row of bins. The twist of paper containing the hack-saw blades lay on top of the rubbish in the bucket. Gus was edging his way in apparent idleness towards him. Solly lifted the twist of paper and showed it to Gus, winking. Gus winked back.

The mouse, deciding to make a dash for it, suddenly darted towards the left. The cat sprang forward, swung a paw, missed, and the mouse, jinking like a rugby player, streaked across the square with the cat after it. Everybody turned to watch the chase.

Solly and Gus reached the bins together, and bending over to empty his bucket, Solly hissed, "Tomorrow night, man. After dark. They will have a car up there in M – – – street." Gus snatched up the blades and they disappeared quickly under his red shirt, clamped to his side by an arm. His heart beat wildly then, and his throat was dry. He thought, wonderingly, What has happened to my nerves? It wasn't like this in the old days. But he was sauntering back towards the shade of the Isolation Block.

The mouse had reached the wall of the platform outside the Headquarters Block, and now, trapped, dashed along its length until the cat reached out swiftly and cuffed it aside, and it rolled back into the sunlight, scrabbling frantically with its tiny claws. The cat flashed forward, surrounded it with its forepaws while it crouched, wounded and panting, feeling the breath of the cat upon it and smelling the harsh felinity.

Gus had dashed into the Isolation Block, up the stairs and into his cell. He clawed the parcel of blades from under his shirt and thrust it under his blanket roll. He was relieved that it was the week-end. The guards would not institute any of their sudden searches on a week-end. He dashed downstairs again, his heart leaping, and drew up sharply at the door below. Then he strolled unobtrusively into the square.

The cat was watching the mouse crouched between its paws. It lay on its belly again, breathing on the dusty-grey creature with the bright beady eyes and tiny panting jaws. The mouse had its body drawn taut into a ball of tensed muscle, waiting for another opening, refusing to give up hope. A clubbed paw reached out and nudged it. To the mouse it was like the charge of a rhinoceros. Pain quivered through the bunched muscles and the hide rippled, but it remained balled up, waiting with tiny, beating heart for another chance to escape the doom that waited for it with horrid patience.

Then the cat made a mistake. It rose up on all fours. Without hesitation the mouse streaked straight forward, under the long belly and out past the swishing tail. There was a vast roaring sound in its ears. It was the laughter of the onlookers.

The cat spun round; too late. The time taken to turn by the cat gave the mouse a few seconds headway and it was off, hurtling across the square again. Something huge and shiny – it was the boot of a guard – tried to block its passage, but it swerved skilfully, and its tiny muscles worked desperately, and it headed into the shade.

The cat was a few inches behind it, but it swerved again and then the blurred, dark hole of a drain-pipe loomed somewhere to its right, seen out of the corner of one pain-wracked eye. The mouse dodged a slashing, sabred paw by a hair's breadth, and gained the entrance to the hole.

The paw struck again, just as the mouse dashed in, raking the slender tail, but the mouse was gone, and outside the spectators were chuckling over the disappointment of the cat as it crouched waiting at the hole.

Inside, in the cool, familiar darkness, the mouse lay panting to regain its breath.

11

By two-thirty in the afternoon the supper had been served, and everybody had been locked up with their slabs of bread and jam and mugs of bitter coffee.

It was funny how one could become bored with a week-end, George Adams was thinking. You worked all week, and when Saturday and Sunday came, you had plans for a really restful week-end. Then you found you wanted to go back to work. Unless there was a meeting, or you had to help arrange a Saturday night hop for raising funds, or had to go from door to door at night, putting leaflets into houses.

But in this place you could be bored every day. After a while the slow track of a ray of sunlight across the floor of the cell became something of major interest. Even a cockroach emerging from a crack was an entertainment. The drip, drip-drip of the leaking pipe outside was a song you could listen to.

Like that cat and that mouse. That had been as good as going to the pictures, in a place like this. That crowd certainly enjoyed it. You were on the side of the mouse, of all the mice, George Adams thought. The little men who get kicked in the backside all the time. You got punched and beaten like that mouse, and you had to duck and dodge to avoid the claws and fangs. Even a mouse turns, someday. No, not a mouse, it's a worm that turns. Okay. But he was glad the mouse had won out eventually, had managed to escape the slashing claws. You were on the side of the little

127

animals, the weak and the timid who spent all their lives dodging and ducking.

Well, that mouse must have been bloody punch-drunk, slap-happy, after that mauling it received. People got knocked slap-happy by life, too, and did funny things. Like that Casbah Kid over there. I wish he'd talk, say something. It would relieve all this waiting. But he's slap-happy. Like he'd been in a boxing ring all his life and was slap-happy from it. Well, he killed a man, didn't he? Deep down, perhaps, he had not meant to kill anybody. But he was punch-drunk and he just out with that knife. Anyway, why doesn't the bugger say something, talk. Bored as hell, and locked up with a slap-happy boy who talked in spasms. I should have asked old Mrs. Isaacs to send in a newspaper every day, George Adams thought. They allowed newspapers for prisoners awaiting trial. I will have to tell her when she comes again.

The Casbah Kid was waiting for Monday. On Monday he would be taken down to the Supreme Court again, and he would be sentenced to death. He had no doubts about that. It was fixed in his mind. Not being able to indulge in any sort of intricate thought, he accepted an idea, good or bad, and it became fixed in his brain, tightly, like a picture pasted in a scrap-book.

He was nineteen years old and all his recollections of life were a series of pictures, shoddy, dog-eared, smudged pictures of dirty scenes. They were all there, in his mind, so he could look back at them, secretly page back or riffle the leaves and see the smutty scenes, like filthy postcards, flash past. If he liked, he could stop at some page and look at a particular picture, examine it, and afterwards pass on or shut the book.

He did not talk about what he saw in the grimy pages of his mind, but now and then some special scene would worry him, as if the page had accidentally become folded or crumpled, causing a bulge in the book; then it nagged at him like a pimple or an aching tooth. But that happened very seldom – there was discipline and orderliness even in the smut – so that the secrets remained with him, available only for his private consumption.

But now there was a fold in the page, and it worried him. The accepted inevitability of the gallows did not worry him as much as this did. The Casbah Kid was thinking reluctantly that perhaps he should tell this man here in the cell with him about it. He half-listened to the dripping pipe. This john was okay, he admitted grudgingly. He had shared his food and had not grumbled when he parted with a cigarette. That made him strange, but at the same time, an all right bloke.

Gus waited for Sunday night. He waited impatiently, and this impatience was surprising him. Prison had worn his confidence, and he had to exert his will in order to hold onto the nerves which had served him during his career as a cat burglar. He had clung to precipitous walls and rickety drain-pipes and had not felt as worried as he felt now.

He thought that if he told the two about it, he would feel better. But they had the rest of that day, and the whole of the next to go, before he put the plan into operation, and he was afraid that they might let a word slip accidentally, or even squeal to the guards. He was not worried about Morgan so much; Morgan was okay, a game john. It was Koppe he was concerned about. Koppe was frightened and might give the whole game away, just to get into favour with the guards.

So Gus lay there on his blankets and scratched himself, wishing that time would pass quickly. It was fortunate that they had fixed it for Sunday. Over the week-end there was not the usual complement of warders on duty, and that gave them a chance. The leaking pipe tapped away somewhere outside.

Gus said, frowning, "Why you rookers so quiet?"

Morgan was sitting up, his back against the wall, and he

said: "They should everybody out to go to the blerry bioscope on a Sarrerday." He grinned. "You got something on your min', Gus?"

"Me? No, man," Gus said.

"You reckon we'll get one year, two year, extra for closing up that white man?"

"I don't give over a damn," Gus said, and then he smiled to himself, discarding his impatience like a cigarette butt, feeling confidence returning again. He would not be around to serve extra time.

"That basket was asking for it," Morgan said reminiscently. "A real pig of a basket. I's sorry I didn't use the spade on him."

Koppe looked up at him. He said anxiously, "Hell, that would *mos* be murder, man."

"So you only die once," Morgan told him. He scratched himself and found a louse, cracked it between thumb-nails. It made a sound like a snapping twig. "Reminds me of a joke I heard, hey. You know, Gus, how these Dutchmen always telling you you bring these things in with you? Is never in the blerry jail when you arrive. No, you bring it in with you.

"Well," he narrated, "there is the Prophet Daniel what the king of Egyp' or Baby-lon or something want to put him in the lions' den, *mos*. So he *does* put Daniel in there, hey. So Daniel stay there the whole night, and the lions don't touch him a bogger. Well, the next morning the king come around to see what happen, and there he find *ou* Daniel still alive with the lions around him, not worrying with him.

"'Morning, Daniel,' the king, he say to *ou* Daniel. 'How did you spend the night, hey?' And *ou* Daniel, he say, 'Not too bad, King. But these lions, they was a little troublesome.'

"Well, the king, he's just like this: 'I's sorry to hear that, Daniel, but you must have brought them with you'."

And Morgan guffawed at his own joke, mouth gaping, showing off the dull gold tooth, while Gus chuckled and said, "Dammit, *ou* Morg, that's a helluva one."

12

A hard breeze was blowing outside, promising to turn into a full-scale southeaster before the day was over. Through it, the sunlight made the usual barred pattern on the floor and on the drab paint where former occupants of the cell had left their epitaphs, salutations and warnings: *Pike is a squealer; God gives us life and the hangman his rope; The Buster Boys was here; Goodbye Molly, I will always remember you.*

The leaking pipe tapped away at its irregular Morse. The hymn-singer had started the morning with Christmas carols and was in the middle of *While shepherds watched their flocks,* as the door was re-locked after breakfast. Nobody shouted him into silence; apparently hymns were allowed on Sundays. The breakfast mush was cold and a skin like flexible plastic had formed over it.

"Bet is yesterday's stuff," The Casbah Kid muttered. "Those baskets not going to put themself out on a Sunday morning." In the Isolation Block the prisoners ate in their cells.

"There's some canned fruit left over from yesterday," George Adams told him. But the boy was shovelling mush into his mouth, swallowing morosely.

"Old lady I'm staying with is sending Sunday dinner," George Adams went on. "We'll have a nice lunch, hey. You got no people visiting you?"

The Casbah Kid looked at him for a second, and then shook his head, his eyes back on the bowl of cornmeal. Just today, and then tomorrow, he was thinking. Today is Sunday, and then tomorrow. Doom advanced on each passing second, with each drip of the leaky plumbing, the sucking sounds of the wind outside. But he flicked the thought away as he did the wet mush sticking to his fingers.

They heard the guard coming upstairs again. Below, the prisoners in the Remand Section were cleaning up, chattering through the splashing of buckets. The guard unlocked the door of the first cell and then came on to theirs, calling, "Okay, all out. Clean up, clean up." He left the door open and went downstairs again, not bothering to wait for them.

George Adams and The Casbah Kid took the latrine bucket and the water urn and went out. The three convicts were just coming out of the next cell and the man with the scarface smiled at George Adams and said, "Morning, pal."

"Hullo, there."

"Listen, don't say I'm rude, hey," the scarfaced man whispered. "But can you spare another fag, mister?"

"Naturally," George Adams smiled. He got out his cigarettes with one hand and offered the box to the convict. The latter looked over the balcony rail and then took four cigarettes, ducking back into the cell with them. He came out again, winking at George Adams and saying heartily, "Sunday. Sunday today, pal."

Prisoners were emptying night-soil buckets into the drains which had been opened in the square. A broom swish-swished over concrete and somebody was crying, "Give way, give way." The guard in the yard was cleaning his nails with a match.

George Adams went to the sink on the ground floor of the Isolation Block to fill his urn. The convict with the flat, dark face was there, running water into his own container, and he winked and smiled, showing the big, friendly gold tooth.

"How you, chommy?"

"Still going strong."

"What you doing in this block?"

"Talked back to *ou* Fatty."

"*Ja*," the dark man said, lifting his urn from the sink. "White man don't like no talking back, hey." He grunted under the weight of the urn. "Don't like any talking back." He went heavily up the stairs, his bare, yellow-soled feet slapping each step. George Adams washed himself at the sink, and then afterwards filled his urn.

132

On the upper floor The Casbah Kid was sweeping the floor of their cell, and when George Adams had placed the water container on its wooden stand, he held a sheet of old wrapping-paper while the boy brushed sweepings onto it. "I'll take it down," he said. "Take it easy, mate."

"You don't have to do it," the boy said suspiciously.

"Hell, don't take on so, man," George Adams laughed. "Sit down, have a smoke." He gave the boy a cigarette and bundled the sweepings up in the paper.

Going downstairs with it, he thought, That lighty must be thinking a man is doing him a favour for a reason. Nothing for nothing. Never came across such a suspicious john. Then he remembered that the boy was one day away from an almost definite death sentence, and thought glumly, Maybe it's because of that. Like doing a man a good turn because he's going to die, like the condemned man's last cigarette.

He went into the square where the breeze caught at him, tugging at his clothes. He carried the parcel of sweepings over to the bins by the grille and dropped it in. Somebody said through the high bars: "Hullo, Professor. Long time no see."

George Adams looked up and there was Yusef the Turk grinning at him.

"Yussy, you sonofabitch, how *are* you?" he whispered, surprised to see the tall, lean man there behind the grille.

"Not too bad," replied Yusef the Turk. "They took me to hospital."

"What the hell did they say?"

"Nothing. Poked me around, likely, took a picture, and gave me some stuff to rub on. But I got to go back tomorrow."

"Hell, man, I missed you, pal," George Adams said, feeling happy now. "What happened about that other business?"

"Ah, they looked around, asked things. Maybe they will keep on until somebody breaks. The hell with it."

"I wonder who *did* kill that Butcherboy, though," George Adams said.

"Same here, mate. Must have been one of his own gang." Yusef the Turk shrugged. He said, "When I came from hospital I heard they took you over for segregation."

"*Ja*. Old Fatso got wild at me."

"– – – – him. Well, I'll look out for you when you get back, Professor."

"Of course, yes, Yussy, pal."

"Safe, man."

George Adams was about to say something else when the guard in the square shouted, "Fall in, fall in. Caps off." So he winked at Yusef the Turk and moved off, looking over his shoulder to watch the tall man limp to where the prisoners were assembling.

They were all down in the square now; the three convicts, and The Casbah Kid and George Adams fell in beside them where they were lined up in front of the Isolation Block.

The door of the Headquarters Block opened and the preacher came out. He carried a large black Bible under one arm, holding it securely, as if it was a briefcase containing important secrets. He was a short, dumpy man with a dry, aging face and white hair like straw pasted down, lying close to his pink skull even in the stiff breeze blowing through the square. His shoulders were narrow and he had a large belly and wide hips, short legs, so that he gave the curious impression of a large version of an up-ended spinning-top. But draped in jet-black frock coat, black trousers and shiny black boots, he looked exactly like what the whole prison had dubbed him: *Skoppenaas*, the Ace of Spades.

He nodded to the guard who held open the gate for him, and bounced like a balloon towards where the assembled prisoners were seated in rows. In front of them, the store boy had set up something like an iron music stand, and had laid a sleeping-mat behind it. Taking his place on the mat, the preacher opened the large Bible on it at a place marked with a black ribbon, and looked for all the world like a choir-master about to conduct an oratorio.

Instead, he bowed his head, expecting the squatting rows of prisoners to follow suit, and commenced to intone a prayer. Few heard what was being said, for the words were caught by the breeze and whipped away. When he had pronounced a sonorous "Amen", he said briefly, *When the roll is called up yonder.*

The prisoners, who had waited dully through the prayer, were ready enough to sing. Sunday service was a break in the routine of their existence within the walls, and as far as they were concerned, they could sing all day as long as there was not too much talk and sermonising in between. So they swung into the hymn with gusto, voices blending expertly into enthusiastic harmony, while the preacher beat time with a finger. Leading the singing with smiling devotion were the followers of the late Butcherboy.

When they had run through the hymn, the preacher produced his spectacles, and peering at the page marked in his Bible, began to read in a professional voice: . . . . *Straight-way in the morning the chief priests held a consultation with the elders and scribes and the whole council, and bound Jesus and carried him away and delivered him to Pilate* . . . .

The crowd listened stolidly to such scraps of the sermon and quotations as the wind left behind, waiting for the preaching voice to reach the end of its dissertation. It was difficult to judge whether the preacher was there out of devotion to his mission of conversion, or whether he came regularly each Sunday merely because he had been picked for the task by his superiors. Nevertheless, the assembled prisoners waited through the words with the bored air of cannibals who had, out of politeness, granted a visiting missionary an audience, and who listened with reluctant patience to his strange message.

When it was over, the assembly sang *Once in Royal David's city,* with their previous enthusiasm, and after-wards Brakes Peterson shuffled forward to request the *ou*

135

baas to lead them once more with *When the roll is called,* that being a favourite among prisoners.

While they sang this last hymn, the kitchen squad arrived, carrying between them the racks laden with bowls of rice and beans, and a finger each of meat.

The guard looked at his wrist-watch, and waited for the preacher to gather up his Bible and leave the yard. The preacher smiled and nodded at the guard and bounced away towards the arch leading to the Hard-labour Section, while the prisoners, lining up to receive the dinner, broke into yet another hymn.

13

Morgan stared in surprise. For a moment his jaw hung limp, like a flap from a broken hinge, then he gathered it up quickly, and cried, "*What?*"

Koppe said, fright bringing a stutter to his voice: "You's m-mad, m-man."

"I will say it again," Gus told them, grinning with pleasure at the surprise he had produced. "We's scraping out of this place tonight, I said."

Morgan was the first to realise that Gus was serious, and he asked quietly, "How we going to do it?"

"You game, *ou* Morg?" Gus asked, peering into the dark face.

Morgan shrugged. "Man got to take a chance, don't I say? If it work, okay. We's out. They stop us, we just come back here, *mos.* More extra time, hey. So?" He looked at Gus. "How we going to do it?" he asked again.

"They'll get us," Koppe intervened excitedly. "They'll get us. No, man, I don't like it. They going to get us."

"Shut up. Hold your jaw," Morgan snapped at him.

Gus looked at Koppe and said, "Listen, pally. Hear me. You going with us, understand? You stay behind and they going to ask you how come you didn't give the alarm when we was scraping. That going to get you extra, in any case. So you can make up you min', you going, hey." He sounded ominous.

"I don't want to go," Koppe muttered. He sounded as if he wanted to cry. "I don't want to go, *jong*."

Gus asked darkly, "So what you going to do? Maybe you going to start shouting for the guard when we start?"

Koppe stared back at him, trapped and hopeless, seeing the menace in the scarred face. Outside, the wind was rising steadily, whistling through the prison. He looked away and said sullenly, "They going to get us, man."

"Ahhh, he'll go," Morgan said to Gus. "He'll go when the time come." He sucked at the gold tooth. "*How* we going to do it, Gus?"

Gus said, "I got saw-blades. We'll start sawing as soon as the guard has finish his inspection."

"Saw-blades? Where the hell you get saw-blades?"

"Never min' that," Gus said. "I got it, man. We got all afternoon to saw through that wire, and then one of the bars. There will be *mos* enough space to get through. From the window, onto the roof. Is easy. We leave the wire and the bar in their places until tonight, after the night-guard come up for his look, understand? He don't come in, and he won't see nothing wrong from the door, don't I say? Then, when he's gone, we move out fast, like. By the time he come round again, we's away."

Morgan broke into a chuckle. "Gus," he said softly, "Gus, you's a smart one to get saw-blades. So you got nice little saw-blades, hey? You work it smart, *ou* Gus. Real smart, awright." He slapped his bare knees in delight.

Koppe sat in his corner, looking scared. He plucked nervously at his lower lip and then started to grind his palms together. He said frightenedly, "They'll shoot. They'll shoot, I tell you."

"Shut up," Gus snarled at him. "You reckon we going to give up this business because of you, you fairy?" He glared at the terrified man. "Listen, if you didn't tackle that guard with us, you wouldn't be here, don't I say? *We* didn't ask you, did we? We rush that white man and there you was, in it with us. Now you got to go all the way, see?" He grinned again. "It worked out nice. Tackle that guard, and so they bring us here. It was work out nice."

Morgan now looked at him, frowning. He asked, "You mean you fix it for us to run that guard, just so they charge us and move us here for the court? Then you had your people send the blades here?"

"Naturally, *ou* mate," Gus replied, smiling. He rubbed his palms together in a gesture of joy and confidence.

"Hell," Morgan said. You could have *mos* told a man. How you then?"

"Well, you know *mos* now," Gus laughed quietly.

"They'll hear us sawing the bars," Koppe said suddenly, hoping that he had found some excuse for abandoning the plan.

"Crack," Gus sneered. "We's upstairs, and we will be singing while we do it. They'll hear the *singing*. You can sing hymns, can't you?"

"Sunday," Morgan chuckled. "White men don't min' hymn singing on a Sunday." He started to hum to himself, *Fishing for Jesus,* and winked at Gus.

The scarfaced man laughed and slapped the other's shoulder happily. Then they settled down to wait for the guard to make his rounds. Beyond the cells the wind hissed and shrilled against the unresisting stone.

14

Mrs. Isaacs had sent George Adams a Sunday dinner: half of a home-baked pie, boiled vegetables, spaghetti and cheese, sliced cucumber, all wrapped in grease-proof paper. George Adams had divided all these carefully between the two of them, and they had eaten everything, except the fruit which had been sent with the food, and had washed down the meal with draughts of milk from a waxed carton. The prison rations they had ignored. The Casbah Kid admitted to himself that it had been one of the few decent meals he had had during his nineteen years of life.

The meal over, they reclined on their blankets like, George Adams thought, Roman patricians after an orgy, but while George Adams felt a little drowsy, The Casbah Kid was seized by a gnawing feeling that the time had come . . . .

To The Casbah Kid, that afternoon meal had been very like the one served to a condemned man, and he considered himself already condemned.

When a dam bursts, a mighty flood is released. If a man is habitually abstemious, liquor will loosen his tongue; when a persistently taciturn man decides to talk, he can be expected to say a great deal. Some men talk under torture; others when they are delirious; still others when they are positive that they are soon to die.

The wind was blowing outside and the afternoon moved on its cautious way towards a gusty sunset. In the cell next door, the three convicts were still singing lustily above the sound of the wind. They had been singing hymns all afternoon.

"Those johns really got the religion," George Adams remarked, and yawned.

"Like a blerry funeral," the boy muttered and gnawed at a thumb-nail.

"Funeral," George Adams said. "They say talking about funerals is bad luck."

"Who's got good luck?" The Casbah Kid said and ground his teeth. "Not me."

"Ah, forget it, man," George Adams said. "It might not turn out so bad. Cigarette? A man don't have to carry his troubles around like a coat." He struck a match and held it for the boy's cigarette, then lighted his own.

The Casbah Kid said, "Well, you not going to hang, mister." He added through a puff of smoke, "I'm not scared, hey. No, I'm not scared of that, mister."

"Maybe it will be okay," George Adams told him, trying to disguise his pity. "Maybe they just send you up for a few years, man."

"No," the boy said. "They going to hang me like they did to my pa." He frowned. "Just like my pa."

The men in the next cell were still singing at the top of their voices.

"Listen," said The Casbah Kid, raising himself up onto an elbow. "They hanged my father for the murder of my mother."

George Adams stared uncomfortably at this boy, as if he had discovered for the first time his bitter and awful presence. God, no wonder he doesn't like to talk, he thought. With that on his mind.

"Your pa murdered your mother? And was hanged?" he murmured, as The Casbah Kid gazed at him with the ancient marbles of his eyes.

"He was hanged *for it*, mister," replied the boy, and the bruised mouth twisted into the parody of a smile. He added, "And I could have saved him, hey."

"Jesus," said George Adams. "You don't have to talk about it, man."

"Listen to me, mister," The Casbah Kid pushed on, ignoring the hint. "When the police bust in it was all clear like – like a picture, see?"

"Somebody living downstairs, below us, she see blood spreading on her ceiling, like. Blood from the room where we live, understand? So she call her old man, and he call the law . . . ."

What was it the police found when they broke in? On the floor of the shabby tenement room, with its peeling wallpaper, musty bed, patched window and the smell of spilt liquor, a woman lay limp and awkward. She was dead, having been stabbed in the throat with an ordinary breadknife which was still in the wound. She lay in a pool of blood, and if she had not been killed outright, she must have certainly bled to death.

140

Seated, or rather sprawled in a kitchen chair, lolling across the table, was a man. He was in a drunken slumber, head on one arm, the other limp at his side, and his unshaven, bloated face agape with heavy snores. An empty bottle stood on the table, another had rolled across the floor to come to rest against the skirting-board. In a corner, flung there like a rag doll, lay the pinched and stunted body of a boy.

He was not dead, but suffering from a savage blow on the head, a broken arm, a blackened eye and various bruises and abrasions. These apart from signs of malnutrition and probable tuberculosis. It was evident, too, that the woman, starved and aged before her time, had been brutally beaten, her eyes swollen and her clothes torn.

As far as the police were concerned, it was simple. The man had come home drunk, bringing with him two bottles of cheap and strong wine which he had consumed in the room. He had savagely assaulted the woman, and when she had fought back, had seized the knife lying close and had stabbed her in the neck. During the course of the fight, or perhaps before it, he had brutally struck and kicked the boy, leaving him half-dead and insensible in the corner. After which he had fallen into a drunken stupor.

"That was okay for the Judge," The Casbah Kid said. "A clear-cut case, mister, like they say."

The convicts next door were still bawling hymns.

"It looked like it," George Adams said, shaking his head in sympathy. "There wasn't witnesses, hey."

"But there was a witness, mister," the boy told him. "Me. I saw the whole thing from beginning to end, *mos.*"

"So you could have saved your pa," George Adams murmured, gazing at The Casbah Kid. "Hell, you could have lied to save him, I reckon. What a helluva thing to be in. Did you have to give evidence against him?"

The Casbah Kid drew up his knees. He bit at the cuticle of a finger. The light had faded outside, and the wind, tearing out of the south-east, drove angrily against the stone walls, then whooped and whistled on its way.

"In the court my father shouted for mercy, screaming that he was innocent. He called on The Man Above to witness that he didn't know a thing about it. He said he was drunk when the law found him, and if he *did* do it, he was too drunk to know what he was up to. He was out of his min', like.

"Then he said, how can he stab her so exactly through the big vein if he was dead drunk, like he claimed he was? But the Judge, he ask him where was the evidence that he didn't murder her *first*, and *then* drink himself drunk.

"So that is where I come in, mister.

"My pa, he ask the lawyer they give him, to call me to talk for him. Okay, they take my evidence, but I talk only up to a certain point, see?

"I told them like this: For so long as I can remember, my old man, he was a drunky and a bully. So many times I have seen him beat my ma without mercy, with a buckle belt or his fists. Sometimes he hit her with a chair. He could knock her senseless with one blow and then kick her while she lay there. So many times, also, he whipped me. Most of the time for nothing, for no reason. I don't know where he got money, but he spent it on wine. Most of the time we had no food to eat. My ma sent me out to beg at people's doors.

"On the night that my ma died, he came home, full of wine, but he could still walk and talk. He had two bottles with him, but no food.

"He demand my mother to give him food. When she told him there was no food, hey, he knock her down, and then he kicked her until she was out. Then he said he was going to give me the same.

"When I try to dodge out of the room, he kick me with all his strength, hit me with his fists, throwing me against the wall. Then he took off his belt. My ma, she's trying to get up and throw herself between us, and he hit her again.

"What I saw after that, I told the Judge, I was not going to tell. So help me, even if they torture me.

"Well, the law, they reckon I don't want to give evidence

to send my father straightaway to the gallows, and they feel kin' of sorry for me, like. So they stick to their own ideas about the crime, understand? Still crying that he didn't do it, my pa is taken down to the cells under the court, while they stop for lunch."

The Casbah Kid was silent, biting his nails and looking at nothing. They heard the door downstairs being unlocked, and the guard coming up the stone steps. The convicts were no longer singing, and the wind roared outside. The guard came down the gallery, looking into the cells, and then went downstairs again. The heavy door slammed and the lock turned with an iron squeak.

"Now look, old mate," George Adams said quietly, "You don't have to go on if you don't want to. Try to get some sleep and forget all about that."

"No, no," The Casbah Kid muttered. "I got to tell it. Tomorrow another Judge will send me the same way my father went. I got to tell it, hey."

He glanced at his bitten nails, and with his chin resting on his knees, said, "Well, I ask them to let me go below to visit my pa in the cell. They feel sorry for me, and say is okay. So I go down to see him, this man what made my ma's life a misery like hell, and who never had a word for me, and did nothing but give me the belt.

"Oh, he was very sorry, mister, then. He cry and ask me to forgive him for all what he did to me and my ma. He cry and snivel and beg me to save him. I'd *mos* seen what had happen, he pleaded. Why didn't I tell them? He was dead drunk, out for the count, he had not done a thing. Did I see him do it, did I?

"'Tell me, old son,' he cried. 'Tell me now, what happen that night.' He shivered and wept and begged me not to let the white men hang him.

"'Hear me,' I say to him. 'Just listen to this, hey. You want to hear what happen, hey? That night? Awright'."

The man slept drunkenly across the table, his wine-laden snores rasping through the stale air in the room. On the

143

floor sprawled the limp forms of his victims, the boy and the wife. The woman recovered first, looked about with pain-drugged eyes, and saw the huddled body of the boy. "Dead," she whispered. "My little child is dead." Then she turned to look at the drunken wretch who sprawled in a stupor across the table.

"I saw it all," The Casbah Kid muttered. "I wasn't dead, of course. I was dazed, maybe, but coming awake. Then I saw my mother drag herself over to the table on hands and knees. He had kicked and hurt her legs so bad. Near my father's head lay the bread-knife with which we was *supposed* to cut bread, but never hardly got a crust from *him*.

"I see her reach up and take the knife. I could have shouted to her I was still alive.

"'But why, why didn't you?' asked my father, shaking with fright there in the cell under the court building. 'Why?'

"'Because why, I thought she was going to kill *you*,' I told that swine what happened to be my old man. 'She was going to murder you, reckoning you had killed *me*. You reckon I was going to stop her? You reckon. So I stay still, making as if I'm dead, in the corner, but I was watching.'

"I waited for her to drive it home, into his neck. She was crying. Maybe she still had love for him. Who knows? But instead of stabbing him direck, she reach for his right hand, open it, and place the handle of the knife in it. I stared, wondering what she is up to. Wondering must I shout or not. No, I lay still. I reckon, happily, she is going to help him stab himself. It will look like he killed himself. That was real smart.

"Then she close his slack fingers around the handle of the knife. Her own hands held it tight as she could. And then she lift up the knife, holding it in his hand, and put the sharp point to her own neck.

"Even as I sat up screaming, 'Ma, ma, *don't*,' she jabbed inwards with her hands still holding his and the knife with his fingers round it.

"'Oh, that damn', dirty bitch,' my father cried, there in

the cell. 'That dirty bitch, she commit soo . . . *soo-cide*. She want to put the blame on me. Oh, the bitch. God will punish her and save me, an innocent man, hey.'

"*Ja*. Thinking I was dead, my ma thought she was coming to join me, to leave my pa, the murderer of her child, to explain away two corpses.

"'My son, my own son,' my father cried. 'Now you will save me. You will tell them all.'

"I smile at him.

"So when they brought him back into the court, he is wild with joy, see. He stood there in the dock, gabbling out the story what I told him. He was innocent. I would tell them everything. He turn on me, shouting at me to tell them what he was telling was the real truth. He was innocent, he babbled, and *I can prove it*."

"And what did you say?" asked George Adams, horrified, as The Casbah Kid ground a finger-nail between his teeth.

"I stood there in the court, mister, and it was as if I saw my mother's ghost rising up behind the Judge. I look at him and I shake my head. 'I don't know what he mean,' I say."

"So they hanged your father?" George Adams whispered. He did not know whether to look upon The Casbah Kid with astonishment, contempt or pity.

"The Judge say he don't accept drunkenness as excuses," the boy scowled.

"But-but," George Adams asked, stuttering. "Is this story true?"

The Casbah Kid looked at him and chewed a thumb-nail.

15

They had been sawing at the wire screen and one of the bars all afternoon. As soon as the guard had come up for his first round of the section, and had departed, Gus had sprung to his feet, eager as a terrier. The guard would not come again for another half-hour.

"Right-o," he had whispered, keeping his voice low in case the two men next door could overhear what they said.

"Now we going to start." He turned to Morgan who had also risen to his feet. "Morg, you give me a lift onto your shoulders, and I'll cut first. Okay?"

"Right," Morgan had said. He entertained certain doubts about the whole operation, but he was willing to take the chance. Morgan was neither reckless nor cautious, but accepted the situation as a fact, and therefore dealt with it accordingly.

The third convict, Koppe, on the other hand, was trembling with fear. He wanted nothing to do with the escape, but the two powerful men intimidated him, and he knew that he would have to go through with it. He had stared at them, and chewed his lower lip to stop its trembling. His heart was bounding like some monstrous spring which had broken loose.

Initially he had stressed his protest: "You johns is mad, mad. They going to catch us, you hear?"

"Crack," Gus had said, going over to his blankets, pulling them aside to uncover the paper-wrapped blades. He had torn away the wrapping and chuckled as he flexed the hacksaw blades.

"Hey, careful, man," Morgan had whispered. "You'll break them, and then what?"

Gus had chuckled gleefully. All his old nerve had returned, and he was certain of success. He wrapped one end of the steel blade in paper to make a handle, and said, "Hup, mate," to Morgan.

The dark man grinned, had crouched and Gus, straddling his shoulders had been lifted up the wall and in front of the window. He had looked down at them. "Okay, start singing."

Morgan laughed shyly, and then cleared his throat. "You better lead off, pal."

"What'll it be?"

"Hell, *ek weet 'ie*. I don't know. Try *Onward Christian Soljers.*"

Gus had started to sing, a little off-key at first, and then straightening out, with Morgan joining with his heavy bass. Koppe stared at them, jerking with fright. Fear was like a palsy in him, and he shuddered, listening to the two men. Gus had stared down at him, snarling as he sang, and then Koppe had joined in, his voice squeaky with alarm and near to tears.

Outside the window, the wind howled and tore at the wire mesh. Gus had driven the narrow steel blade through one of the tiny squares of the screen, high up on the side, and started to saw.

The tiny teeth of the blade had cut into the metal, rasping above the sound of the wind and the bawling of their voices. They had finished the hymn, and the blade had cut downwards, through two inches of the wire. Each drive of the blade was like the thrust of a phallus, and each parting of a hard strand, an orgasm of metal. Gus had swung into *Stand up, stand up for Jesus* and his arm worked to the rhythm of the marching hymn.

Later he had climbed down, and he had given Morgan a turn. They had not bothered to include Koppe in the sawing, but had forced him, with threats and curses, to sing louder, and his quavering voice had supported theirs, shakily, with its feeble accompaniment.

Each time, during the afternoon, when they had heard the door below being unlocked, they had returned quickly to their bedding, where the patrolling guard had found them singing hymns to themselves.

At one stage, during *When the roll is called up yonder,* the first blade had snapped, and they had stopped singing while Gus cursed and got out another. His right forefinger had been worn raw by the bite of the thin steel, and he sucked it again and again during pauses in the sawing.

All the time he had been worried that the rest of the blades would snap before they reached the bar, but the second blade had held, and as time passed they had sawn, taking turns, right down the side of the screen to the window-sill.

After that there had been no need to lift each other. They had brought the water urn on its stand over to the wall under the window, and had stood on its lid, spelling each other, sawing horizontally along the line of the sill.

They had sipped water whenever they grew hoarse from the singing, and all the time they had kept on sawing. The blade ground through the squares of wire, the sound of its path now drowned in the hymn singing and the hooting of the wind.

Koppe had not watched them working. He sat on his bed on the floor, and sweated with fear as he sang. Once when his voice had trickled away like a spring running dry, Gus had kicked him viciously in the ribs with a hard bare foot. He wished the guard would appear silently and discover the plot. Perhaps they would let him off lightly, since he would only be sitting there, not participating in the break out.

But the guard had not come, and Gus and Morgan sweated from their exertions at the window.

Then Morgan had cried, "That's him, that's him." Looking up, Koppe had seen that they had sawn all the way across the width of the screen. Morgan's gold tooth glowed brassily as he grinned, and Gus had slapped him jovially, winking and chuckling.

Then Gus had remembered the four cigarettes given him by that fellow next door, and he had got them up and had generously presented Morgan with one whole one. Morgan had a few split matches secreted in his clothes and they lighted up while taking a break.

Gus had looked at his hands, the hard-labour callouses on his fingers worn through by the saw-blades. "Well, that's *mos* worth-while wounds, don't I say?" He grinned, the knife-scar slackening like limp string on the side of his face.

After several puffs, Gus had pinched out his cigarette, but Morgan had passed his to Koppe, saying, "You better fan away all the smoke, mate. And don't look so – – – – ing sad."

"Blerry fairy," Gus had said. "Damn fairy." Sneering at the slight man who puffed nervously in the corner.

Then they had returned to work on the window. Gus had lifted the flap of wire screen gently so as not to bend it and leave a noticeable dent or crease, and Morgan had passed a hand through the opening to work on the bar. There were four narrow iron bars set in a vertical row in the concrete, and they had estimated that if they moved one at the end of the row, there would be enough space for a man to squeeze through.

They had all started to sing again, and Koppe, looking sullen, fanned the air with a blanket to drive out the smoke while he squeaked away at the hymn. Outside, the wind lashed and scoured the walls, and the day had drifted into twilight.

When the last light had faded from the wind-swept sky, the bar was finally cut through about an inch from where it sunk into the wall. Gus and Morgan left the severed rod intact, had carefully arranged the wire screen so that, from the doorway, no damage, no line which the hack-saw blades had made, could be noticed. Without careful examination, the assault on the window would remain undetected.

Gus had rubbed his hands together, smiling triumphantly. They were ready to go. He had not mentioned that a car would be waiting up the street on the east side of the prison. It was his car, and as far as he was concerned, the other two would have to look after themselves once they had gained the roof.

"Well, *ou* pal," he had said happily. "That's that, hey."

"Gus," laughed Morgan, "Gus, you's a basket. Getting those blades in here was smart, real smart."

"Well, we can relax, pal, until the time come, hey."

They had retired to their respective blankets and mats to await the night-guard.

16

The heavy iron key ground in the lock of the metal-clad door below, the heavy padlock, for extra security, clacked shut, and the guard went off across the half-lit, windy square.

Now Gus and Morgan sprang to their feet and made for the window. They had another half-hour before the guard came around again, and by that time they would have to be gone, not only from the cell, but beyond the walls.

Gus climbed onto the water urn which they had carried back to the window from its place behind the door, as soon as the guard had left, and ripped open the flap of wire screen that covered the window, bent it upward to leave a gaping triangle. Then he grasped the severed bar with both hands and pushed.

Koppe watched him with an expression close to horror. There was something he could do, he thought. He could scream and yell for the guards, shouting that the other two were escaping. They might reduce his sentence for assisting the authorities. But Koppe knew also that it was quite unlikely that he would live to see the outside, after such an act of betrayal.

The half-world of the prison had its own justice. Here in this country of stone and iron the subtle agents of vengeance moved with infinite patience, and the orders of retribution were carried in the mysterious diplomatic bags of the grape-vine, from cell to cell, from outpost to outpost, from prison to prison. So that even if he was sealed in the deepest dungeon, he knew that at some time or other they would get him. Even if he was released unharmed, he would never be safe.

So he stood there, shaking with fear that was like a stone in his belly, while Gus bunched shoulders and biceps and thrust the bar outwards. The iron bent under the power of muscles made hard by work in the quarries, and in a few seconds there was an unguarded gap in the window.

Gus thrust the bar outside, so that it could be used as a step in the climb to the roof. He looked down at Morgan and winked. He said, "I'll go first. Send the fairy after me and you come last, *ou* Morg. That's the best way. I'm not leaving this squashy behind to make a row."

"Okay, mate," Morgan said. Gus having arranged the escape was entitled to go first, and naturally they couldn't trust the other man to come last. "But you better make it quick, hey."

But Gus had already heaved himself up into the opening between the side of the window and the remaining bars. For a moment he crouched in the narrow space, grasping the escape bar for support.

Opposite him, across the small, dark kitchen yard, was the back wall of the Administration, windows dark. To the right, the staff quarters. Light glowed behind curtains on the upper floor, a little above the level of the Isolation Block, and Gus stared with beating heart at the windows. But nobody appeared at them. Below him the kitchen yard was dark and silent.

He heard Morgan hissing behind him, and he straightened carefully, edging sideways through the window, peering upward. The wind caught at him, tugging at the old red shirt, and he clung to the bar. A little way above was the parapet around the roof of the Isolation Block.

He was all right now. He was back on the old job; a traveller returned home. He grinned in the windy darkness, and then, holding a bar with one hand, he reached up against the rough, peeling wall with the other, balanced carefully outside the cell. He raised a leg and placed a bare foot cautiously into the curve of the projecting bar. Then he heaved himself quickly upward, his weight on the bar.

Gus felt the bar give a little, but before his entire weight could force it down, his free hand reached the top of the parapet, hard, strong fingers clutching like a grapnel. The other had released the window and swung upwards, and for a moment he had all his weight on one hand, feeling the twinge as the muscles of arm and shoulder stretched taut. Then the other hand was on the parapet, and he was heaving himself upwards, clambering skilfully onto the roof.

The wind howled and roared across the roof, slapping into him, stinging his eyes. Gus crouched at the wall and looked over. Koppe's face and upper body were just emerging from the cell window. Gus saw the man's terror-filled eyes gleaming in the patch of light from the window as he hovered there, over the kitchen yard. Behind him, Morgan would be urging him on, cursing softly. For a moment Gus wanted to leave them behind and make a break for it at once.

Below him, Koppe shivered with fright, one foot already on the bar, a hand clawing upwards. The wind wrestled with him, trying to pluck him from the wall and blow him like a scrap of paper into the dark yard below. He wanted to scream in fear. He wanted to release his precarious grip on the bar, fling himself down into the darkness, end all this terror and panic. He shut his eyes, his teeth chattering. Then he felt Gus's powerful grip on his upstretched wrist and felt himself being hauled angrily aloft.

Koppe's bare toes scrabbled at the peeling distemper of the outer wall. He reached the parapet, clawing with his free hand. The edge of the concrete-work jarred his breastbone, scraping away the skin and he babbled with pain. Then he was wrestled onto the roof, hearing Gus cursing through the screech of the wind.

"Come on, come on you sonamabitch," Gus snarled, the words disappearing into the blustering night. Koppe crouched shivering behind the parapet.

The next moment Morgan came up over the wall, the whites of his eyes like pieces of chalk in his dark face.

Gus was already moving off across the corrugations of the roof, into the bawling darkness. He crouched low, moving like a cat on hands and toes. He made for the corner of the roof where the narrow arch joined the roof of the Remand Section. Beyond the Remand Section were other roofs, a sprawling pattern of squares and rectangles formed by the cramped subdivisions of the prison.

He reached the corner, and peered over, eyes narrowed against the lash of the wind that thundered out of the south-east to claw at the prison walls, at the rooftops, at him. To the right was the square where they exercised, and to the left the bigger yard of the Hard-labour Section. Lights, fixed into the walls, behind panels of plate glass, threw an insipid glow over the tarmac. The yards were deserted; the guards probably in another part of the prison on their patrols. In front of him the top of the rectangular arch stretched across the gap between two buildings.

Cautiously Gus rose and peering quickly to left and right, drew himself onto the narrow gangway. Lying flat, he dragged himself slowly across. The wind grabbed at him, held, pushed and pulled, and for one awful moment he thought he was about to be blown into space. But he reached the other side, after what seemed an infinity of time. He slithered over the parapet onto the next roof.

He glanced back. Behind him Koppe was scrambling frantically across the archway, his mouth agape, eyes bulging. Gus cursed him in the racketing of the gale, motioning down-down-down with a hand. But Koppe came on, exposed as a ship in full sail against the wind, and reached the other side.

Koppe saw Gus's mouth opening and shutting as he swore, but the words were spun away. Then Gus turned and was off, crouched behind the low parapet of the roof of the Remand Section.

Koppe threw himself flat on the roof, feeling a stab of pain where the corrugated iron bumped his scraped chest. He had recklessly exposed himself on the archway, driven on by fear, and now fear urged caution, and he clung to the riffled metal, dragging himself slowly along on his stomach, through the smell of bird droppings and cold metal, his whole body jiggling in terror as the wind tore away above him. He knew that now that he had committed himself to the project, he would have to go through with it.

Morgan crossed the archway safely and huddled behind the wall. He looked about him in the blowing darkness. Gus was out of sight and he caught a glimpse of Koppe crawling painfully away into the gloom, a blurred shape like a giant crab.

Morgan was neither afraid nor excited. Of stolid character, and endowed with the knack of accepting situations as they arose, he moved out across the roof with the one thought of getting the matter off his hands.

Above him the darkness writhed and undulated with the wild, vast caresses of the south-east wind, and the starlit sky, dark purple, glimmered like a blanket strewn with cheap jewellery. Away, beyond the outer walls of the prison, the city glowed like a dying bonfire in the night haze, and along the harbour front the silhouettes of cranes rose like the dark, uncovered forms of petrified monsters.

The back of the block formed one side of a square. The other three sides were made up of a two-storeyed Hard-labour Block, a line of store-rooms and a row of lavatories and a shower-room which fronted the coal yard and the Pox Section. An iron grille in a corner of the square led to another part of the prison.

Now, peering over the wall behind which he crept, Gus saw the guard unlock the grille and come into the entrance to the Hard-labour yard. Re-locking the gate behind him, he strolled down the four steps to the asphalt. The guard wore a greatcoat and cap, and had a rifle slung from one shoulder. Gus watched him stroll into the dim light from the wall lamps, slapping his keys against the skirt of his coat.

The guard stopped in the centre of the yard and looked around. In another corner of the yard was a big tank which contained disinfectant. Next to it was the barred gate to the Hard-labour Block. The guard walked over to the gate and tested the lock. Then he turned and looked upwards, along the lines of the roofs above him.

Gus did not know whether or not the guard saw his face peering down. But when he saw the guard's face turned upwards, his nerve broke like a rotten string, and before he could control himself, he had leapt to his feet and was tearing along the roof in a panic.

The guard saw him and yelled. At the same moment he unslung his rifle and raising it, fired. The muzzle blast of the .303 made an orange-yellow aperture, which lasted for a second in the half-light of the yard, and the sound of its detonation, partly snatched away by the wind, was a quick, flat, snapping crack. The guard yelled again and then was running towards the alarm switch in the wall opposite him.

17

"But was that story *true*?"

George Adams gazed curiously at The Casbah Kid who sat there, knees up, gnawing at a blunt finger-nail.

This was the first time that The Casbah Kid had considered tearing a page from the murky book of his mind. He had felt like doing so and exposing it to somebody, before they took him up to the Capital to hang him. This thought he had thumbed around in his mind. It had been like trying to decide whether to confess some hideous sin to a priest, or to surrender a few trivial misdemeanours and slink off with swindled absolution. But now, withdrawing once more into himself, having shown the page, he decided that this bloke wanted to know *too* bloody much. So he looked at George Adams, his eyes both sullen and sly.

And, he's a bloody mystery all right, George Adams thought hopelessly. Slap-happy, that's what he is, man.

For another second The Casbah Kid's eyes had brightened, as if he was about to reply to the question the other man had put to him, but then they heard something which interrupted. Their heads cocked, listening

From somewhere in the whistling darkness beyond the block came a shout, then the crack of a rifle, and the next moment the siren on top of the prison cleaved the windy night with its strident blade of sound.

George Adams was on his feet in an instant, his eyes wide with excitement. "Christ," he cried. "Somebody's escaping."

He sprang to the door, craning his neck to look out through the window opposite the gallery, but all he could see was a rectangle of night.

The siren wailed on, its metallic ululation rising and falling through the wind. They heard the guard fire again. Then the shouts of other guards running across the square below, reached them through the window. Afterwards came another sound of gun-fire, a flat crackle of many shots, and George Adams thought, It sounds just like a cane being whacked on a table-top. Then he was aware of a new sound.

It was an uproar caused by hundreds of shouting, chanting voices punctuated with the clamour of hundreds of metal mugs being banged against iron doors and stone walls in an irregular, cacaphonic chorus. The prisoners were jeering the warders, singing, and cheering on the escapees.

The solidarity of the underworld, George Adams thought, with a smile. He listened to the uproar and heard the harassed warders rushing around with threats of "No break-fast. Meals off, meals off" unless the demonstrations ceased.

Somebody fired again, and then again, and voices of guards yelled orders against the wind and the jeers of the confined prisoners. The siren kept up its wailing.

It occurred to George Adams that no sounds came from the next cell. He strained his ears and heard nothing along the balcony, and he told himself with surprise, Why, it's those blokes who have got out.

He turned to The Casbah Kid, excitedly. "Hell, those johns next door. They broke out. Jesus, right under our blerry noses, too."

"Good luck to them," the boy acknowledged grudgingly. He was still tensed on his bed, wrapped in his own grimy thoughts.

After a while the sound of the siren dropped, hesitated, and then faded away completely, leaving the racketing of the wind to accompany the uproar in the cells.

Guards were still shouting, and then a man boomed defiance, and another voice screamed and screamed. The door below slammed open and footsteps pounded upstairs. George Adams, peering down the gallery, saw a group of guards, three of them in uniform and another in holiday shorts and sports coat. The fifth man was the Superintendent. He wore his pyjama jacket under his mufti, and he was red-faced and furious, his bony body shaking with rage.

A guard unlocked the door of the middle cell and they went in. They came out again after a few minutes. The Super was looking at pieces of hack-saw blades which he held in his skeletal hand, saying angrily, ". . . . these *bliksems* get them? How did they get them?" They all went down-stairs again, without looking at George Adams at the other door.

Somewhere below, a man was screaming, begging for mercy, and then the screaming reached the ground floor of the Isolation Block. A guard was shouting, "You black devil basket." Then the sounds of blows and kicks and the soggy sounds of boots into flesh. Somebody groaned in agony, and another voice shrieked and begged.

A guard shouted, "Where's those blerry chains?" Beyond them, from the other cell blocks came the jeers of angry prisoners.

George Adams left the door and went over to his bed. He looked at The Casbah Kid and said, "They got them. Those – – – – guards got them."

But the boy was already drawing up his blankets, composing himself for restless sleep.

18

It's all over, Morgan thought, there on the roof in the dark, with the wind clawing at him like a frenzied woman. He heard the guard in the square below fire again at Gus's fleeing shape and then the shriek of the siren severed the night near him.

Behind him, a window of the staff quarters, almost level with the roof, was flung open and a guard leaned out, holding a rifle, his eyes scanning the darkness.

Below, other warders were tumbling out, shouting and pulling on coats, holding pistols and rifles. From all over the prison rose bedlam.

The guard at the window saw Morgan, raised his rifle, aimed across the intervening darkness, and fired. He worked the bolt and fired again. While he fired, he was shouting, "Stand still, you bastard. Stand still."

Voices yelled, "They're on the roof. Get a ladder. A ladder."

Armed men were clambering onto outhouses and projections of which there were many inside the old prison.

Morgan heard the bullet crack over his head. He knew that silhouetted against the sky, he was a reasonable target for the guard at the window, and he did not want to die. So he straightened, turning as the guard fired again. He twitched with fright as the shot grazed his cheek-bone and whisked past his ear, but he recovered instantly, flinging his hands high, standing still, dead still.

"Awright, don't shoot, you mucking baskets," he shouted, not without defiance. His deep voice boomed through the wind and the howling of the alarm.

Somewhere else, away from him, a burst of gun-fire popped like a string of firecrackers, and he wondered whether they would get Koppe and Gus. The guard at the window was shouting, "Walk forward to the edge of the roof, you – – – – *skolly*. Slow, or I'll blow your head off." Morgan caught only snatches of the words in the noise of the wind and the siren, but he guessed the orders, and walked slowly forward, arms aloft. His cheek burned where the bullet had grooved the skin, and he could feel the warm blood trickling down into his neck.

He reached the parapet and looked down, covered by the guard at the window. In the yard, guards were wrestling a ladder into position, others waving revolvers and truncheons.

"Down, you pig, down, come down," somebody shouted at him.

"Awright, I'm coming down, you baskets," he roared back, swaying like a dark tree in the wind. "Your mothers, you pigs of sons of bitches and baskets."

He cursed them all the way down the ladder, unloading the invective upon them with the stolidity of a farmhand shovelling dung. So when he came within their reach, the guards clubbed him with truncheons and gun-butts and kicked him insensible with hard-toed boots while he crouched, taking the pain that exploded in his hard, tough body, while he continued to curse them, until he leaped into unconsciousness in a searing white light.

Please God, don't let them kill me, Koppe prayed on the roof of the prison. Fear knotted his bowels and he was sweating in the chill tug of the wind. Please, please, My Lord, they are on the roof and they are going to kill me. My Own Lord, do not let them shoot me, please, please, please.

Terror froze him to the roof, so that he could not stand up to surrender. He had scrabbled wildly over roofs, through the darkness when the siren had started, and he now lay against a parapet, shivering with fright. He did not hear the siren, or the wind or shouts and the gun-fire, but felt only his fear. He had not wanted to escape, he thought. Those other men, Morgan and Gus had forced him to do it. He would tell the Law that they had made him do it.

He was weeping in abject terror. He wanted to get away somewhere, to hide, to run, to give himself up, to die and forget all this awful, consuming fear which gripped him.

After a while, Koppe raised himself, trembling, and peered over the parapet against which he crouched, and discovered, to his astonishment, that he had reached the outer wall of the prison. Below him, a twentyfoot-or-so drop away, was the dark and deserted street.

Gus, too, had reached the outer wall at another part of the prison. He had fled across the expanse of rooftops, leaping connecting walls and projections in a desperate rush for freedom.

Guards were bringing ladders to scale the walls, and he heard their shouts. Once they caught sight of him, weaving like a whippet and a crackle of gun-fire had followed him. He heard the shots whip around him and his heart leaped with terror. But the thought of friends waiting nearby to carry him away to safety, maddened him and drove him on.

The wind ripped at him, clutched at his clothes, screeching like an evil spirit intent upon his downfall. He tore on, bare feet pounding the metal of the roofs.

Now he had reached the end of that section of the rooftop, and there, across a narrow alleyway, rose the top of the outer wall. He crouched, panting, on the edge of the roof, steadying himself for a moment in the wind, and then sprang.

His hands clawed at the sharp top of the wall, gripped and held. His bare feet scrabbled madly, and he hauled himself up. He gained purchase on his elbows, feeling them scraped skinless by the rough summit of the wall. He swung a leg up, desperately and gashed the knee. Then he was on top of the wall. Gus drew himself up, poised on aching feet in the darkness, for the leap downwards into the street.

For a second he teetered on the wall, and then a great gust of wind shrieked at him, swept him as easily as it would a leaf, back into the prison.

Gus fell with a bubbling cry of despair, and then screamed as his hip struck the ground, jarring him with pain. He was aware of people crowding around him and he screamed again as a guard booted him viciously in the ribs. Somebody else clubbed him across the shoulders with a truncheon, and he shrieked again and again, crouching, grovelling at their feet.

"This is number two," a guard shouted. "Where's the other one, you *bliksem*? Where's the other one?" And they struck him again, hearing him scream. "Where's the other one?"

"No, no, no," Gus wailed, weeping with fear. "I don't know, boss. *Ek weet 'ie, baas.* I don't know."

They hauled him to his feet and a fist smashed into his face. Clubs, fists, boots pounded him while he wailed and wept. Begging them not to beat him, they dragged him away.

At the Isolation Block, they were unlocking the iron door of The Hole. Morgan lay groaning on the floor in the corridor, while a warder slipped the chains on him, locking the waist-band and snapping the manacles shut around each ankle. While they were chaining Morgan, other guards came up with Gus, slapping and kicking him, while he begged and pleaded. They shackled him, working angrily, and he babbled and wept, kneeling with chains heavy from waist to ankles.

Then the guards flung them both into the black confines of The Hole and slammed the heavy door.

A long time afterwards, Morgan came out of the darkness of insensibility into another darkness – the darkness of a sealed tomb. He emerged slowly out of unconsciousness, groaning with the stabbing pain that racked his body. There was blood in his mouth and all over his face; his eyes were swollen into great, aching bulges, and his bones ached. He lay there in the solid darkness of the punishment cell, and allowed himself to recover. Later he put his fingers to his mouth and wiped blood from his gums, and spat. Surprisingly, his gold tooth was still intact. He hawked and spat again, and shouted hoarsely into the blackness.

"– – – – you all, you sons of bitches."

He stirred cautiously, wincing, and chains clacked and rattled. In the harsh darkness, somebody was weeping, a bubbling, gulping sound. Morgan turned painfully onto his side and grunted. He kept his eyes shut for it hurt him to open them, and in any case he would be able to see nothing there in the womb-like blackness of The Hole.

He whispered, croakingly, "Gus? You there, *ou* Gus?"

Chains rattled and clashed, together with the wet snivelling. Morgan asked again, wincing each time he moved his mouth to talk, "Gus, you there? *Ou* pal. Where's that Koppe, hey?" He was not even sure that is *was* Gus, there in the dark with him. It might even be that fairy, Koppe, who was crying.

But then Gus's voice whimpered back at him, painful and frustrated. "The basket got away. He got away, – – – – him."

"Away?" Morgan muttered. "Him? Got away?" He was silent for a while, listening to Gus weeping. Then he giggled. He giggled again, and the sound went on for a while and then developed slowly into painful laughter.

Morgan laughed and laughed, oblivious of the pain it caused him, his body shaking, and the chains clink-clinked through the high, hysterical, neighing sounds. He lay there in the dark and laughed in a mixture of hysteria and merriment.

"What the – – – – you laughing for, hey?" Gus whined. "What the hell you laughing for, you basket?"

"Got away," Morgan hiccoughed. "Got away. *Ou* Koppe got away. *That* fairy." He shook with laughter that hurt him all over. "Why man, that little basket didn't even *want* to go."

Morgan lay there and filled the darkness with his crazy and painful laughter.

19

A guard came out of the Headquarters Block and hammered on the iron triangle. The wind had died away, and it looked as if it would be another hot day. The sky was pale, washed-out in the warming dawn; a flock of pigeons, flying in haphazard formation, streaked off and over the prison, headed towards the sunrise.

On the upper floor of the Isolation Block, George Adams woke up out of a dreamless sleep. He was surprised, because he had expected to be troubled by nightmares after all that excitement and cruelty. He sat up on his blanket and yawned, fisting his mouth, and looked across to where The Casbah Kid was also throwing off his covering. Then George Adams remembered, with a surge of remorse, what day this was. He thought, I'm not going to press him about that story of last night. Better leave him with his troubles. He looked sadly at this strange youth, and said nothing.

They got up and folded their blankets. He looks a little pale this morning, George Adams was thinking. Or am I mistaken? Maybe it's just because I know what he's facing.

The Casbah Kid was quiet as they went downstairs to be included in the count, and to wash; he looked sullen when they had to wait for the bowls of mush.

The officials had not carried out their threat of withholding breakfast, and over in the yard the prisoners were forming up to receive their rations. Everybody was chattering excitedly, discussing the events of the night before. George Adams saw Yusef the Turk, and gave him a thumbs-up sign.

While they were all waiting, a squad of guards arrived and went into the Isolation Block and along the ground floor. They unlocked the door of The Hole and shouted at the men inside to come out.

The square fell silent as the two convicts were escorted out, limping between the guards, their chains dragging at waists and ankles. They had swollen, blood-stained heads and faces and clothes. The dark man had a gash across his cheek and blood had dried and caked on his clothes. But he sneered with swollen lips at the guards, showing the dull gold tooth as if it was a flag of defiance.

The guards took them away towards the dispensary, and the assembled prisoners watched them go. There were armed guards stationed on the roofs of the prison now, and seeing one of them standing with slung rifle looking down into the square, George Adams thought, It's like locking the stable after the horse ran away. One of the convicts had escaped, and he remembered a slight, sullen man with the shivery air of a wet pup.

Before they went upstairs with their mush, George Adams obtained some hot water, and in the cell he stirred up some cocoa. He divided the brew into their mugs, and said, "It'll cool while we eat this porridge."

"Don't want to eat nothing," the boy said, changing his mind about breakfast, and George Adams saw the bony look in the prisoner-of-war face.

"Well, have some cocoa, pal. Look I made it nice and strong."

"You got a butt for me, mister?"

"Naturally, man." George Adams got out his box and gave The Casbah Kid one. Then he said, "You better take a few. Sitting around all day without tobacco is lousy."

The hymn-singer had started to sing *All things bright and beautiful.*

"T'anks," The Casbah Kid said, and took three more cigarettes from the box. He put them in the pocket of his shirt and lighted the first one with the matches George Adams handed him.

"You better keep the matches, too," George Adams said. "I got another box in my coat pocket."

"Okay."

Jesus, George Adams thought, It's like the bloody firing squad again. He did not watch the boy as he sat on his pile of blankets and rolled mat. The Casbah Kid drank some of the cocoa between puffs at his cigarette. He smoked a little nervously, but the thin hand holding the mug, did not tremble, and his face maintained its stony look.

Outside, the clerk had started to call the names of those due to appear in court that day. They listened to the names, and The Casbah Kid tightened the laces of his old gym shoes while they waited.

Then he rose and went to the door and George Adams rose too, and The Casbah Kid shouted down through the wire screen and the bars: "That's me. Here I am, upstairs."

He turned back towards George Adams and the bitter mouth, with the wispy moustache across the upper lip which

164

was not too swollen now, grinned with its usual reluctance. He licked at the lip and seemed to think about something, then he wiped the palm of his right hand on the seat of his jeans and then stuck it out with a jerky, almost embarrassed motion, as if shaking hands was a strange gesture to him.

George Adams took it and smiled at the boy. "Good luck, mate."

"Okay, mister."

The door downstairs was unlocked and the guard came up the stairs, saying, "Albert March, Al-bert March."

Without releasing George Adams's hand, The Casbah Kid looked over his shoulder and said, "*Ja*. Here I is, in here." Then he looked back at George Adams, hesitated and said quickly, "I must go now."

The guard unlocked the cell and The Casbah Kid let go of the other's hand, stepped past the guard. George Adams stood there in the cell, alone with the scribbled walls and the drip, drip-drip of the pipe that leaked somewhere.

20

Having been sentenced to death, The Casbah Kid clinched his armour of silence tight about him. Standing there in the dock, with the smell of polished mahogany and the whirr-whirr of electric fans, he shut himself off from the alien faces surrounding him: the solemn white face of the Judge under the coat of arms, the pink faces of the blue-uniformed police and the faces of the Prosecution, and the Defence who had been appointed for him by the court, and who was quietly gathering together batches of papers. He did not belong here with these white faces and neat suits and spotless shirts; only the clink of keys at the bottom of the steps to the cells was familiar.

The Judge, sentencing Albert March to death, chose to make a speech.

The reign of terror due to knife gangs which prevailed

could not be tolerated any longer, he stated. And the courts, by imposing the most severe penalties, should do their part in helping people to live a peaceful existence.

"Repeatedly from the Bench, references have been made to the wave of stabbing affrays in parts of the city and the country," he said.

"The activities of gangs and individuals who roam around with the knife as their companion can no longer be tolerated. The State and local authorities are involved in immense expenditure in improving social conditions. The efforts to allow people to live better lives are being undermined by elements, such as the one before the court, who have established terror and confusion.

"It has been advanced, on behalf of the accused, that he comes from a class and from surroundings where violence and drunkenness are an everyday occurrence. This cannot be accepted as an excuse."

21

George Adams saw him again that evening when the guards brought him back and locked him in the cell at the end of the gallery in the Isolation Block. They had given The Casbah Kid a new white canvas uniform, stiff with filler and sharply creased along the folds as it had lain in the store. His face, glimpsed through the wire screen before he entered the cell to wait until they fetched him again for removal to the Capital, was shut tight.

Standing at the door of his cell, George Adams saw the convict who had come with the guards, carrying on a tray the boy's supper of soup, boiled vegetables and buttered bread, which they usually gave to ordinary white prisoners.

The guards went away, leaving a Coloured warder, in khaki uniform and topi, on the gallery to watch The Casbah Kid. They did not want condemned prisoners to hang themselves in their cells before reaching the official gallows.

The warder stood at the cell at the end of the gallery for a while, looking in, and then he came down to where George Adams stood.

"Hullo," he said, sounding friendly enough. "All alone?"

"*Ja*," George Adams replied.

"Well, you not *that* kind of lonely," the warder said, motioning with a thumb towards the end of the gallery. He sighed and shook his head. "What people don't *do* in this world, hey."

He sounded as if he had made a discovery.

"How is he?" George Adams asked.

"Look awright. Don't say nothing, though."

"He got a cigarette?"

"Oh, they give them a ration of tobacco."

"You better give him some from me," George Adams said to the warder.

"Okay. I reckon is awright. You know him?"

George Adams nodded. "Yes, sir, I know him. He's a pal of mine." He passed three cigarettes through the screen to the warder, who took them down to the cell. He came back after a while and said, "Just quiet."

"When they going to take him away?"

"Later on. Train going north tonight."

Then the door below was opened again and the warder went away. The Superintendent came upstairs, accompanied by a head warder. They went to the door of The Casbah Kid's cell and looked in. The Super slapped his bony thigh with his swagger-stick, and said, "March? Is this March? March, are you awright?"

George Adams did not hear whether or not the boy replied, but the Super said: "You'll be going away just now, hey. From now on you got to keep your eyes on the Man Up There. Just keep your eyes on the Man Up There." He paused, and then said, "Hmmm."

Then they went downstairs again. Outside, the wind was starting to rise again, and George Adams could hear it whispering secretively through the cell blocks and the outhouses of the prison yards. The lights glowed pallidly inside the cells and from the walls of the deserted squares.

George Adams was still at the door when the guards came again to take The Casbah Kid away. He watched them through the wire screen and heard the heavy lock clack and squeak.

The Casbah Kid stepped coldly out of the cell to join the guards. He felt uncomfortable in the stiff new uniform, and the hard edge of the collar scratched his neck. He looked expressionlessly at the faces of the men who waited to take him downstairs. He paused for a second, and then brushed past them, going down to the cell where George Adams waited.

George Adams saw the boy come up. The guards made no move to stop him, and George Adams saw him on the other side of the wire screen. Fingers with bitten nails touched the screen, and for an infinitesimal instant there was a flicker of light in the cold, grey eyes, like a spark of faulty electricity. The bitter mouth cracked slightly into one of its rare grins.

"So long, mister," The Casbah Kid said.

George Adams nodded. He said, "So long, mate."

Then the boy turned away and went back to the guards and George Adams watched them all go downstairs. The door below slammed shut and the lock grated, leaving him alone again, with the scribbled walls, the smell of tobacco and blankets and the chuckling sound of the wind.

The next morning they moved him back to the Remand Section.